The Stars We See

Book Two: A Heart that Dances Series

J.P. Sterling

Contents

Chapter One

Gabby dropped a tote the size of a small bathtub on the floor in front of me. "My line of credit has been frozen again." Her breath was heavy like she had just ran down the block. "They said I went over my limit, but when I checked, it looks like one of my vendors rang in my order wrong and double-charged me."

"Do you want me to call them?" I was still unsure of what my job duties entailed. It was my first day of work as her assistant and I had only been in the office for five minutes. I had done some research on assistant jobs, and from what I had read, I assumed I would spend a lot of time in the office reading emails, answering calls, and setting up appointments. I knew I wouldn't be given headship over any major responsibilities because of my lack of experience, but I was excited to get a chance to dress cute every day. Like today, I went out of my way to find the perfect deep-emerald wrap dress with a professional Johnny collar, pairing it with a matching pair of peep-toe heels.

"I'll call the vendor, but it takes days for credit refunds to go through. My rent is due tomorrow and I've already been late twice this year. My landlord said he'll evict me if I don't pay on time." Gabby removed the lid off the tote, revealing dozens of marigold scarves. They were in new condition, all sealed individually in plastic bags. I recognized them as the same scarf I had fallen in love with last year when I had visited.

She picked up one of the sacks and ripped it open. Then she yanked out the scarf and practically heaved it at me. I caught it and held it awkwardly in front of me, not knowing what I was supposed to say or do. "I need cashflow like yesterday," she went on. "I already clearanced these out on my website, so I'm hoping orders start coming in, but until then, I need you to sell as many as you can." She put the lid back on the tote and then looked back at me. "What are you waiting for?"

I watched her dead-serious expression, which scared me from asking questions as to *how* I was supposed to sell them. I casually smoothed my perfectly groomed low ponytail back. "Um, how much do you want me to charge?"

"Whatever you can get." She crossed over to her desk, scouring the surface for something. "That reminds me, you need my payment information. You can take my tablet with the credit card app for anyone who wants to pay with credit." She found the small tablet, neatly tucked away in the case, and handed it to me. "My password is on the inside flap."

I took it from her and tucked it inside my purse. My eyes fell to the enormous tote at my feet. "Um . . . Do you have a cart?"

"I do." She pointed to the wall where one was folded up next to the mannequins. She was already dialing her phone, which told me she was finished with our conversation. I loaded up the tote and headed out the door, not sure of what my plan was to get rid of the scarves. She trusted me way more than I trusted myself. While she waited on hold, she called to me, "There's a loading elevator on that end of the hall." She pointed to the opposite direction of how I had arrived. "I'm sorry to push you out the door so fast on your first day. It's baptism by fire in this job."

I forced a brave smile. "It's okay. It'll be fun. I love this sort of stuff." Then I moved the cart down the hall in search of the elevator. This task reminded me of a reality show I'd seen on TV where people were hired to do a job they had never done and one person got fired every week until there was one person left who got hired. I knew I couldn't get fired or I'd have to go back to Montana, and I couldn't stand another year there with my parents. I had to find a way to sell these scarves to prove I could do this job.

I struggled to get the cart over a small step at the building's exit. Then I wheeled it to the edge of the curb and removed the lid. Scanning the oncoming pedestrian traffic, I located my first potential buyer. "Excuse me, ma'am." I approached her, holding a scarf out in front of me. "Would you like to buy a—" She didn't even look my direction and kept walking.

I spotted another woman and timidly smiled at her, but she looked away. I needed a different approach. I took the unwrapped scarf and styled it around my neck, pulled out my phone and took a selfie. Kicking myself for not having social media, I went with the next best thing and texted Tina and Becky.

Abs: *Hey girls – I'm at my first day of work and I need to sell these scarves. Can you post this picture to your social media? Tell them they are Gabby's and are on special price today. I can deliver them!*

Becky: *Sure :P*

Tina: *Why are you wearing a winter scarf with that dress?*

Sighing like I had just got sent to detention when I read Tina's text, I tapped my fingers on the cart handle, trying to come up with a solution.

It would be awesome if it started to snow right now, I scanned the blue-gray sky. I had no idea what I was doing but I did know standing still not talking to anyone was not going to sell anything. I was in the fashion district with a cart full of fashion I needed to sell. Pressing my feet hard on the concrete to propel the cart, I plunged forward, determined to make this happen.

I stopped in front of the first boutique, opening the door with one hand and pushed the cart inside. There were several sales associates working; some were on the floor with customers and one was behind the counter. "Hi," I greeted the gal behind the counter.

"Welcome," she replied.

"I'm an assistant for Gabby Rue, a fashion designer here in New York. I have some scarves I'd love to show you to see if you'd be interested in selling them in your store." I waited for her to smile, but she didn't.

"I know Gabby," she stated without looking at the tote.

"She's great." I unwrapped the scarf I was still wearing and held it in front of me. "These are all hand sewn and in a great mustard neutral that can be worn with so many colors —" I stopped talking when she shook her head.

"Our buyer isn't here right now, so you'll have to come back."

"I can do that." I glanced at the clock on the wall. "What time do you expect her back?" I asked, but then a customer tried to come up to the counter to pay but couldn't get around my cart. "Here, excuse me," I said to her. I shoved my cart back, but unfortunately smashed it into a rack, succeeding in causing two dresses to fall to the floor. I leaned over to pick them up and whacked my head on my cart handle. Rubbing my head with one hand, I rehung the dresses and looked back at the lady. "Did you say she was coming in today?" I asked, trying to sound casual.

"She won't be in today. You can come tomorrow, but I honestly don't think she'll buy those. She knows Gabby, and her stuff's so expensive that we can't mark it up enough to make any money." She gave me a dismissing facial expression and started ringing up her customer.

"I'm offering a fantastic deal. It'll be a great chance to get a new product in with very low risk to you." I held out the scarf to her. "Would you like to try this one and see how it feels?"

"I'm not much of a scarf person." She leaned over the counter, scribbled something on a pad of paper, then tore the sheet off and handed it to me. "Here is the name of our buyer with our number. You can call tomorrow to see if she's here." Her eyes glared at my cart. "So you don't have to wheel that thing down here again."

"Thank you. I'll do that." I forced an enthusiastic grin on my face. *This wasn't working either.* "Thanks for your time." I yanked at the cart that was now stuck on something. When I tried to free it by giving it a shove with my foot, I caught a glimpse at my brand-new pair of peep-toe heels I had proudly slipped on two hours ago. I had convinced myself I'd be sitting behind a desk all day and I wanted to look cute. These shoes were already starting to pinch my toes and it wasn't even noon. The cart jerked forward, and I was moving toward the door. I desperately tried to act cool and called back, "Have a great day!"

As soon as the door shut behind me, I cringed with embarrassment at how badly that went. I needed a new plan. I didn't want to call Gabby to admit I was failing on the first day. I called the one person I knew who could sell anything.

"Dad."

"Hey, Abs, how's it going?"

"Not great."

His voice lowered with concern. "Didn't you start work today?"

"I did." I sullenly pushed my cart forward as I talked. "But I have no idea what I'm doing. Gabby asked me to sell these scarves because her bank accounts are frozen and she needs money, but I don't know how to sell them."

He was quiet.

"Dad, are you there?"

"Yeah, I'm here. I was listening."

"I tried asking people on the street, but they are mostly walking away from me, and I asked Becky to post a picture on her social media, but I haven't heard anything back."

"Walking up to people on the street is never going to work because it gives the customer the power. You have to lure them to you," he said.

A guy walking toward me, carrying a coffee cup, bent forward like he was going to dump his coffee in my tote. I reached my hand out to stop him. "Don't! That's not a trashcan."

"Huh?" Dad asked.

"Someone tried to dump their coffee all over my scarves."

"You have the scarves with you?"

"Yeah, I'm pushing them on a cart."

"I bet that looks attractive." I could hear him chuckle, amused by the visual I had given him.

"I'm trying," I defended.

"I know you are," empathy flowed from his voice. "What did she say about when she needed them sold? Do I have time to get you some graphics you can send out, so you don't have to push a cart around?"

"No, she needs them now or she'll be evicted."

I heard my dad sigh deeply. "Gabby has always been one who works well under pressure."

"What should I do?"

"Okay, I have an idea, but I want you to know I'm only going to do this one time because it's your first day and I want you to get off to a good start with Gabby."

"Deal. I'll do anything. Whatever you say. Just please help me sell these scarves." I held my breath, scared of being embarrassed again, but my spirits lifted as I connected the details of the plan he had laid out. My dad was a marketing professional, and he knew exactly what to do. I felt my chest relax a little, knowing that my dad was now on board. Not only was he always successful, but his support gave me the confidence boost I was desperately needing.

Chapter Two

About an hour later, a could-be-model with mahogany-colored hair and alabaster skin approached me and held out her hand for me to shake. "Aubergine?"

"That's me. You must be Monica?" I knew the name from the years my dad spoke about his coworker, but I never pictured her looking like she belonged on a fashion runway.

"It's nice to finally meet you." She shook my hand more firmly than I had expected. "I worked so closely with your dad for so long, I feel like I got to watch you grow up." When she smiled at me, her face got even more striking, showing off her high cheek bones.

"Thank you for meeting with me. I really need help," I admitted.

She glanced at my tote with a stark expression, then she looked back at me. "Do you mind if I do a little prep before we go on camera?"

"That's fine," I agreed, feeling insecure already in my failures, but tried to stay positive that my dad's plan would work.

"Okay, so we don't want this in the camera view." She motioned to my cart. "It's not a nice enough display to make people want it because it's still in the freight stage." She pushed it back against the building. Then her eyes flashed over me. "You have a great camera face, so you'll do great. I'm going to interview you. Follow the script your dad gave you, but we want the interview to sound like a casual conversation about Gabby's brand. Talk to me like you would talk to your neighbor and you're not really worried about making the sale. Tell me how you love this product and want to help me by telling me all about it." She reached into her bag, pulled out a brush and handed it to me. "Go ahead and freshen up. You can't underestimate what a quick brush and fresh gloss can do."

I took the brush and ran it through my low ponytail and then gave it back to her. Remembering I did have my favorite plum-perfect lip gloss, I dug into the bottom of my cross-body purse to find it and then applied a thin layer and stowed it back in my bag.

"Okay," she went on, "in about two minutes my assistant will be here to record our interview. It's going to live stream to our website and then I'll send it out in an email blast to all our subscribers. You'll have millions of people see this. How does that sound?"

"It sounds like I'm getting nervous." I burrowed into my upper lip with my bottom teeth to stop myself from screaming, but I then remembered the gloss, so I ran my tongue along my teeth to make sure they were not stained.

"You're going to do amazing," she championed. "Stick to the script your dad sent, smile, and look like this is the happiest day of your life."

I let out a hard breath, hearing my heartbeat getting louder. "I think it's the scariest day of my life."

"No, the happiest." She put on a ginormous smile and pointed to it until I mimicked her. Her assistant arrived, ready to record and she counted down from three using her fingers. Perfectly on cue, Monica sprang into action. "Good afternoon, friends, I'm here with Aubergine from Gabby Rue Fashion, and we are live in Times Square with a total transformation makeover giveaway so special you're going to want to stick around to the end of this video to get in on the action. But before I get to that, let me introduce you to my new friend, Aubergine."

I could see her assistant adjust the camera, and I knew I was being recorded. "Good afternoon, Aubergine, how are you?"

My mouth felt like it had a ball of playdough stuck in the back. I was used to dancing in front of thousands, and I loved that attention, but I was never comfortable speaking in front of people. Talking was something totally intimidating to me. I knew I had to sell these scarves, and now that my dad was helping me, I didn't want to disappoint him either. I dug deep like I used to before a dance recital, forced myself into a calm pose, and said, "I'm excited to be here with you."

"I can't wait for you to tell me about this giveaway, but you have something with you I want to check out first. I've been eyeing this scarf all morning and I have to try it on, if you don't mind." She casually took the scarf I was holding.

"This is amazing!" She held it like it was the most precious silk she'd ever touched, and she lovingly caressed it to her cheek. "Can you feel how plush and luxurious this is?" She looked at me, but I was dumbfounded by her expert performance. She lifted her eyebrows, reminding me to talk.

"It truly is, Monica." I stumbled to find the words from my rehearsed script. "This has been my favorite since I first saw it, and it's very special to Gabby too."

"You were telling me about it earlier and it has a phenomenal story. I can't get over what this scarf has done. Tell us about why this scarf is truly more than a scarf."

"Absolutely. It's a great story. I love that I get to work with Gabby every day and be a part of this story that is really, truly saving people's lives. If you zoom in on her logo—" I smiled at the camera while I pointed to her gold heart logo "—at first glance, you see a pretty heart logo, but after hearing her story, you'll see it's a mission statement. Gabby made the commitment when she started her company to care more about people than fashion. Now, she loves clothes and fashion is her heart—" I pointed to the heart again "—but she had an eye-opening experience where she got to see how most clothes are produced by low-wage workers in other countries who were literally starving as they worked. She made a commitment to care about those workers and she fought to pay her seamstresses the highest possible wages and provide them with regular breaks. She's creating a movement and setting a new standard in fashion with this scarf and she can't wait to share it with you."

Monica started stroking the scarf around her neck like it was a long-haired cat. "I love that story. She's not just an amazing fashion designer but a great person. I'm so in love with this, and I want one right away. How can I get it?" "That's another cool thing about Gabby. She wants to meet the people who love her fashion. So, we are hanging out in Times Square today, ready to meet you and hear your stories. I have a limited number of scarves available on a first-come-first-serve basis."

Monica held up her hand to pretend to interrupt me. "I have to stop you; these are not going to last long, so what if I'm not in the neighborhood but I need this scarf?"

"Great question. You can go to Gabby's website and order them now. Again, the supply's very limited."

"It's limited and so worth the cause, and it's gorgeous fashion." She said the word "so" like she was about to start drooling.

"I couldn't agree more," I said.

"And now . . ." She held up her hands like she had discovered she won the lottery. "Tell us about the giveaway and what Gabby's going to do!"

"Yes, everyone who purchases a scarf today will be entered in a draw to win a fashion makeover with a dress from Gabby's elite Gold Couture line. It's a brand-new line she will be launching at fashion week."

"So, I could win a custom-designed dress made by Gabby just for buying a scarf?" Monica let her mouth hang open like she was in shock.

"That's exactly right. Anyone who buys a scarf today will be entered in the drawing."

"I'm sold. When are you choosing the winner?" She leaned closer to me.

"We are keeping the giveaway open for twenty-four hours, and we'll draw a winner live on Gabby's social media tomorrow."

"So, you only have twenty-four hours to get a scarf, but I wouldn't wait long because it's not going to last." She looked at the camera for her final sales monologue. "Get down here to see us in

Times Square or hop online to find one on Gabby's website. This scarf is to die for. I know what I'm going to be wearing this year at my son's football games." Her eyes found me again. "What's the final detail you need to tell me about?"

"If you can come see us in the next half hour and get the chance to grab one of these scarves, I'll have an extra special bonus for you."

"Oh, what's that?" Monica's voice held an inquiring tone.

"You have to buy a scarf to find out." I pretended to zip my lips.

"Alright, I'm getting my scarf right now." Monica shifted her gaze to the camera again. "That's all the time we have, and we look forward to seeing you here or hop online and drop a hello in the comments on Gabby's social media after you pick up your gorgeous new scarf." She paused and smiled until her assistant motioned the camera was off. Then she turned to me and said, "That's a wrap. I hope it helps."

"Me too," I said. I was beyond apprehensive to see what was going to happen in the next twenty-four hours, but for the first time all day I was also sort of giddy, wondering if maybe I could actually pull this off.

Chapter Three

After a redemptive afternoon where I somehow—to my astonishment—sold all my scarves, I ran hurriedly back to the office both relieved and thrilled to tell Gabby the great news. As soon as I walked inside, Gabby looked up from her computer and cheerfully reported, "We are officially out of scarves. I put them on backorder on the website and I have at least a thousand orders in the queue."

I grinned sheepishly. "So you're not too upset about the dress I gave away?"

Her icy-blue eyes widened. "Upset? My website orders are up over two thousand percent. I want to hug you."

My shoulders *finally* caved in relief after a tense day of extreme stress. "It was my dad's idea," I confessed. "He said a giveaway would be better than discounting the price. He said discounts make people think something's wrong."

Her eyes flashed recognition. "I should have known this was Cole's plan." She sunk back down on her chair, looking pleased.

"I was desperate, so I felt like I had to call him. I couldn't sell anything, and I didn't want you to think I'd fail you."

"About that," she started, "I'm sorry I put so much pressure on you. I honestly was having a panic attack."

"It worked out."

"I'd say. Do you know what it costs to have a PR company do a live remote in Time Square?"

I shrugged, still feeling the day in the tightness of my back. "My dad never said. Monica said she owed him a favor."

She refreshed her computer screen and watched the sales numbers jump another notch. "I can't believe what I'm seeing. The orders are piling in, but I have to get these packages out now." She rotated her chair to face me. "Can you help me package and ship them?"

I lifted my heavy eyes to the stacks of totes against the wall. I had planned on being done with my workday. It was past five o'clock; I was exhausted from being outside in the heat with heels, pushing that cart all over town. My feet were pulsing as I fumbled for words, "Sure, I'd love to." Then I turned back to glare at the mountain of freight that now had become my bedtime lullaby.

"I'll print off the invoices as they come in. If you can start unpacking all the boxes, we can start an assembly line here." She pointed her petite finger to a table she had set up with a stack of folded boxes.

I instantly got overwhelmed when I surveyed the boxes, the packets of tissue paper, and the invoices. "You do this all by yourself?"

"No, not usually." She flexed her first box into shape and pressed the security tabs down until they held. "I have a freight gal who comes in. Her name is Sanita, but she won't be in until Friday. Normally, I don't have this many orders, but I don't want to get behind, because next week is fashion week. I'm already sweating about that, and now that my orders are backed up, I might need to hire some temp help."

I kicked off my heels, finally giving up on looking cute. My feet were in survival mode, and I needed to push through this marathon. I reached for the top tote and placed it on the floor in front of me. "Extra orders are a good problem to have," I reassured her, and opened the tote and saw a smashed pile of scarves, all individually wrapped. Then I picked up the first scarf, ripped off the plastic, and looked back at her. "Now what?"

"Now you wrap it in tissue paper and tape it and seal the paper with my gold heart sticker." She took the scarf from me and demonstrated by folding it neatly in the tissue paper, taping it, and placing it in the box she had made. "Then the box goes into a mail envelope with the printed address label on and the invoice inside it." She retrieved the stack of envelopes and invoices resting on her desk. While she was there, she refreshed her computer screen again and her lips curved up. "I love these numbers." She peered at me over her screen. "I'll keep printing these off and get the envelopes ready and you keep stuffing the boxes."

Stealing a glance at the clock, I confirmed what my growling stomach already knew as it was almost six o'clock now. I had several text messages, so I quickly peeked at them while Gabby was busy at her desk. I had a few from Tina and Becky who saw my live social media blast, one from my dad checking in, and another one from Fulton, who also wanted to see how my day went. I desperately wanted to text Fulton back but didn't want Gabby to see me on my phone. I slipped a fast look at Gabby, who was still printing, but she looked like she was about to stand up, so I stashed my phone and grabbed another scarf.

"You hungry?" She lazily stretched her arms behind her, lacing her fingers together to deepen the pull.

I was so hungry I could have eaten one of the scarves. "A little," I confessed as I worked with a sense of urgency while she watched because I wanted to impress her, hoping she'd say I had done enough for the day.

"Why don't you order us some Chinese food? I'll treat us tonight since you had such a great first day." She smiled sweetly at me like she knew I'd appreciate the offer, but it was annoying because I didn't want to take a working dinner. *I wanted to go home.*

"Sure." Biting my tongue, I slid my phone out again, wishing I could call my friends instead of ordering food. "Do you have a place you like to order from?"

"There's a China Wok place downstairs in this building that's great. I'll get a number three with rice."

I scrolled through the numbers on my phone, pressing send on the China Wok. While I waited for them to answer, I tried to sound cool and asked, "So, how late do you usually work 'til?"

"It depends," her voice floated up from behind her computer. "With fashion week coming up, it's not unusual to start pulling all-nighters."

Luckily for me the person on the phone picked up so I didn't have to pretend I was happy about not getting any sleep. I ordered our food and got right back to work.

"I bet this has been a long day for you," she said while reading her computer screen.

I didn't want to act like I didn't appreciate the work, but I was wiped out. "I'm starting to feel it but happy to be here."

"If you want to finish that stack of invoices, you can leave after that. I'll start a new pile for you to do in the morning."

I eyed the pile. It had to be at least fifty invoices. I was not a mathmagician, but I quickly estimated that if I could package one scarf every five minutes, which was working at a sprint pace. I'd be here another five hours! I picked up the pace more as I ripped through the plastic wrap, freeing another scarf. I was slowly realizing Gabby's dream of providing family friendly work hours to her staff didn't apply to me.

I worked diligently until the food was delivered, finally sitting for the first time all day. As glorious as it felt to take a load off my throbbing feet, I wasn't going to waste a hot second and I ate while I continued to tear plastic off scarves, careful to not get food on them. I thought eating would give me the energy kick I needed to get through my stack, but it only succeeded in making me tired. My body moaned each time I reached up to grab another tote from the stacks.

Underneath the dim yellow studio lighting, my eyelids became weighted, challenging me even more to keep my tired eyes open. When I finally slid the last tote from the first stack next to the table, I celebrated with a happy dance, elated that this was my last tote of the night. My body must have felt it too because I couldn't stop yawning. Soft tickling caressed my bare foot. Reasoning I'd dropped a plastic bag, not wanting to stop my momentum, I kicked it away and kept powering through the boxes. After a couple seconds, the tickling resumed in the same spot but this time it felt more like a crawling sensation, and it appeared to be moving up my leg. Then I freaked! *It was a roach.*

"Ah!" I jumped off the floor onto my chair, clinging onto the back of the chair with a death grip, pulsing my leg back and forth, trying to shake off the ginormous cockroach. Gabby jolted, bolting over to me. First, her eyes alerted toward me doing the crazy leg dance on my chair, then her eyes moved down, scouring the floor. Dozens of cockroaches poured out from a hole in the wall and now covered the floor!

"That tote must have been blocking the hole." Gabby frantically pointed to the wall where they were all beading out from.

"We got to plug it back up!" I screamed. I gave up kicking as that ninja roach had super glue legs, and I grabbed a piece of cardboard and used it to scrape the roach off my leg. "Ek!" I shrieked as I accidentally touched it for a few seconds before it dropped to the floor. "I'm terrified of those things. Keep them away from me!"

Gabby speedily slid the tote until she had it pressed back against the wall, blocking the hole. "We're going to have to kill them."

"Can't we call someone?" I pleaded.

"I can call the building manager about the hole in the wall tomorrow, but we can't leave them out like this. There's nobody else here." Her brows lifted with an air of amusement as she apparently wasn't deathly afraid of them like I was. "It's you and me against them."

I tried to muster up some bravery as I looked for something to whack them with. I grabbed a heavy catalog from the shelf. "Can I use this?"

"Go ahead." She watched with an entertained look while I dropped the heavy book on a bug, but it wasn't heavy enough, and the bug crawled out like he was bored. "Step on the book after you smack 'em," she suggested.

I whacked another, stepped on the catalog, and hopped on it a couple times. When no bugs crawled out, I removed the book to find a smooshed roach corpse saturated in bug fluids. I scraped it off the floor with my cardboard piece and dropped it into the garbage. "We need an exterminator or some spray so they don't get the floor all messy."

"I don't have any. The only thing I have is a fire extinguisher," Gabby offered.

It was tempting, but I knew that would make a bigger mess. I pulled out my phone. "I'm sorry, this is one thing I can't do for you. They terrify me, but I'll get help." I pressed send on Fulton's name. "I'm calling a friend to help and telling him to bring some spray."

Chapter Four

It was almost midnight when Fulton walked me the four blocks
to my dorm. My heels were past the point of blisters and were
now completely rubbed raw. My voice was hoarse from screaming,
and I was extra jittery from the epic roach battle we had finally
won. Fulton was amused as he chortled, recalling the night's many
humorous moments. "That was too funny when that one fell on
your arm. The look on your face—" He held his stomach like it
hurt from laughing.

"I'm glad this is fun for you." Flashing an exaggerated fake smile,
I stated frankly, "I'm going to have nightmares for the rest of my
life."

"At least I don't have to wheel you home in a wagon this time."

"I wish you had a wagon for you to pull me home in. My feet
hurt so bad," I half-joked but despite my horrendous night, I
was starting to feel uplifted, grateful for how Fulton had basically
jumped at the chance to be there for me tonight. We were
obviously able to pick up our friendship where we had left off even
though we hadn't seen each other in months.

He sighed, like he was finally able to resist laughing. "Now, I have to go home to study for my biochemistry test tomorrow."

"I'm sorry I stole your study time." I felt a tinge of guilt build in my chest. Up until now I hadn't even thought I might be interrupting Fulton from something he had needed to be doing.

"It's okay. It was worth it to see you in battle mode." His shoulders shook as he tried to stifle another laugh.

"When did you get to be such a funny guy?" I sneered, remembering him always being more serious.

"Not sure. But I know it's been good to get off the farm. You'll see. Once you get away from that place for a while, you will loosen up too." He brushed his eyes over my way for a mere second before returning them to the street and added, "And I think it's helped me to live with Wally. He's taught me to look at the funnier side of things and not take life so seriously."

Grateful the conversation was now off me; I eagerly continued this topic, "You're living with Wally again this year?"

"Yeah, we all requested the same roommates because we got along well last year. You'll have to come over sometime to see what I mean. He's hilarious."

"I know he's funny. I had lunch with him last year because you had a lab, remember?"

Fulton leaned his head to the side, like he was confirming his thoughts. "I forgot about that." He gestured toward me. "So, you know what I mean."

"He's pretty crazy."

"Did he tell you he has his own comedy show on Wednesdays?"

I pursed my lips, noting my throat was still dry from all my recent screeching. "He said he was part of a show."

"Wednesdays at nine. You should come with us this week. We always go."

We had arrived at the doorstop of my building, and I halted my steps. "That would be fun," I said, feeling flattered that Fulton would include me with his friends. "Text me the info. I'll meet you there." I shifted toward him to say goodnight, and for the first time all night, I got to really look at him because I wasn't frantic and trying to avoid the creepy crawlers. There was still a silly sparkle in his eyes that wanted to laugh, but I knew he was holding it in to spare me further embarrassment. He appeared the same as I remembered but there was something different about him that hadn't been there before. It was like a light-hearted echo that glowed through his facial expressions, revealing true contentment that he had been missing in Montana. *The city had been good to him.* Seeing that made me hope it would be good to me too. After my first day of work, I wasn't so sure, but I hoped I had made the right decision to come back too. "Thanks for rescuing us," I said. "I think if you wouldn't have showed up, I would've ended up passing out and been eaten alive."

"Nah, they're not meat eaters." His lips quivered slightly, but then in a quieter, controlled voice he added, "It was my pleasure. I'm glad I got to be there for you." His irises softened, making the silly sparkle dissipate. Taking a step toward me, he planted his feet on the sidewalk just a hair closer than what would have been normal for us. His lips parted, but he never smiled when he said in a low voice, "Thanks for calling me."

"No problem . . . Erg." There was something about the way he looked at me, that made me self-conscious about the fact that I had been sweating in the streets all day and never really had time to freshen up. It was not uncomfortable in anyway, but it also didn't feel typical for us. If I had to attach a singular word to describe it, the only thing I could come up with would be *magnetic*. A shiver ran up my spine, and I shook it off, blaming it on the cool city night. Then I cleared my rusty throat and said, "Hopefully, next time I can call you for something fun."

"That would be nice. I missed you," his words sort of lingered in the air, like he was just as surprised by them as I was. I sort of hoped he'd keep gazing at me like that, but instead he tossed his head to the side and said, "I better get going."

A little disappointed he was leaving so abruptly, I edged toward the door, and agreed, "Yeah, me too. I'm shot. Text me on Wednesday, okay?"

"Okay. Night." He waited to leave until I was all the way inside my building. Then once I saw him walk away, I silently squealed, *What the boloney sandwich was that . . . I missed you . . . all about.* I peeled off my shoes, noticing the insides were stained from feet sweat, worse than anything I had ever smelled in my ballet shoes. Gagging, I turned my head and muttered under my breath, *"That's disgusting, Abs. No wonder he had to leave."* Then I carried them as I dragged my bare feet across the cold, tiled floor. I leaned heavily on my door, fumbling in the dark to unlock it and then finally found my way inside. Paying no attention to where I dropped my shoes and purse, I crossed the room, and finally did a grand finale collapse facedown into my pillow on my unmade bed.

When I groggily returned for work the next day at eight, Gabby was already perched at her desk, steadily working. "Good morning," she greeted me. "I'm glad you came back."

I scanned the floor for creepy creatures. When I was convinced they were gone, I cautiously inched forward. "Morning. How are you?"

"Amazing," she said in a singsong voice. "I have another whole stack of invoices from this morning." She pointed to a pile of envelopes while she wiggled in her chair with a happy dance. "I got a hold of Sanita, and she's coming in later today to help out with the website orders. So, you can focus on getting the scarves out."

I had already accepted my fate of packing scarves all day and was lifting a tote from the top of a new stack, careful to tiptoe around the tote on the floor that was plugging the hole in the wall. "Did you get a hold of someone about the roaches?"

"I left a message for the building manager." She motioned to a store bag on the floor. "I also came prepared with four cans of bug spray."

"Wow . . . What time did you get up this morning?"

"I laid in bed for a couple hours, but I don't think I slept. I've had insomnia for years. Plus, I was worried about my vendors."

"What's wrong with them?" I pushed the tote across the floor, swung the lid open, and pulled out my first bag from the fresh pile of scarves. By now I was used to the concentrated scent of formaldehyde that filled the air every time I worked on freight. I had learned the warehouses sprayed it on the clothes to prevent bug infestations. At first, I had found the smell irritating, but after the ordeal we had with roaches, I both appreciated the effort in using it and also found it comforting to know that it would be unlikely for me to find more crawling bugs inside the bins.

"Nothing. I had canceled the production contracts because I wasn't selling the scarves I had, but now I have so many backorders, I need to have more made. I came here at three so I could get a hold of someone on the phone over there."

"You've been here since three?"

"I have." Her eyes—way too perky for this time of the morning—flashed a look at her appointment book on her desk. "I also posted on my social media a reminder we're going to do a live drawing for the winner of our makeover at one today. We can do a random draw thing with this app I found. I downloaded all the names. We'll have to add the new ones at noon when we do the cut-off."

I was going through the motions of making boxes and stuffing them with scarves as I listened to her narrate the schedule of the day. My ears perked when I heard the word lunch, but I immediately deflated when she finished the sentence with details of a working lunch here in the studio. It wasn't that I didn't appreciate the job, but I wasn't expecting it to be so many hours. I needed some clarity on our arrangement. "So, I was curious as to what sort of coverage you're needing from me as far as hours."

"You can have as many hours as you want." Her voice was sort of monotone and her gaze fixed, reading an email. I was hoping for an answer more specific as to what number of hours I needed to get a week so I could know how to plan things, but as I watched her eyes locked on her computer screen, I knew not to press the issue.

"Good grief." She threw her hands in the air like she was giving up.

I dropped a stack of sealed envelopes into one of the freight totes near the door. I was terrified to ask what was going on because I knew it would somehow influence my job duties. "Everything okay?"

"No." She hurriedly stood in such a manner it caused her rolling chair to drift backwards. Her perfectly manicured hands scoured the desk, loading her purse with a tape measure and a clipboard among other things.

I kept my eyes on my scarves, not wanting to slow down but I did ask, "What's wrong?"

"One of the models I'm using for fashion week—who is amazing, and I used her for the last three years and I have never had an issue with her—just emailed me. She's pregnant. While that's great news, she can't stop puking and she said she's super bloated and gained four pounds since her dress fitting and she's worried her dress will be too tight." She took a long sip of iced water from a glass water bottle that had been sitting on her desk, then closed it and dropped that in her purse too. "It's always something. Sorry to bail, but I gotta run. I need to meet her at the photo shoot she's doing today for a quick remeasure." She flung the door opened, obviously on her way out and then looked back at me. "Are you going to be okay here?"

I dreadfully looked at my stack of invoices and replied, "I think I'll be able to keep busy until you are back."

"Good. And remember, Sanita's coming in and she knows how to run the invoices, so have her print off the ones that come in when I'm gone."

"Got it." I sealed another envelope.

"Oh, and the mail guy's scheduled to pick up this freight sometime this morning. Make sure you get a receipt."

"I can do that."

"Okay, I'll hurry back." She clicked the door behind her, and I was left alone in her studio with only my thoughts and hundreds of scarves left to package. Glancing at my phone, I found a text from my dad, still wondering how my day had gone yesterday since I never called him back. I decided I was due for a break and called him.

"Hey, how's it going?" his voice was boisterous, but I knew he was somewhat forcing it to cheer me up.

"Good."

"I talked to Monica a little. She thought the marketing blast went well. Did you get the sales you needed?"

"We did. We're swamped. I have so many scarves I need to send out, and since Gabby was so slow, she doesn't have anyone but me on staff. I packed freight most of the night last night so I'm *exhausted*."

"That's good you're keeping busy."

"Yeah, I haven't had much time to sit down. I was actually going to ask your advice on something." I put the phone on speaker and set it on the table while I unwrapped.

"Sure, what's up."

"Gabby hasn't explained to me how my hours and breaks work, and I don't know how to bring it up. I don't want her to think I don't want to work hard, but I worked until midnight last night."

"I don't think there's anything wrong with being frank and asking her. I think she's just so used to being a workaholic she didn't realize you were wanting regular hours. Maybe frame your question in terms of wanting to meet her expectations. She'll understand you want to know what she expects."

"I'll try . . ." I sighed, still not convinced that asking again would get a clear answer. "It's been crazy. It's fashion week next week so she's, like, not even sleeping. I had no idea her job would be so demanding." I heard footsteps stop in front of the door and keys digging into the keyhole. "Oh, I gotta go. Someone's coming." I clicked end on my phone before my dad could respond and stashed my phone away in my purse right when the door opened. Sanita, a stout woman with dark hair and cherry cheeks, strolled in, carrying an over-sized plastic soda cup with the straw still stuck between her lips as she noisily sucked out the last drops of her drink.

She smiled at me when she saw me knee-deep in plastic bags. "You must be Aubergine."

"Hi, nice to meet you." I stopped for a moment and shook her hand.

Her smile instantly faded when she saw my stack of envelopes waiting to be mailed. "This is not the way you do this," she scolded as she reviewed the top envelope.

My heart stopped. "What did I do wrong?"

Her chubby finger underlined the label Gabby had prepared for me. "You printed the invoice on address labels and stuck them on the outside. You can't mail these."

My heart slowly started to pump again when I realized it wasn't my mistake. "Gabby labeled the envelopes for me. I'm just stuffing them," I squeaked out, already scared of this woman.

She dropped the envelope back into the tote with an obvious air of annoyance. "You have to redo these. They're all wrong. Gabby doesn't know how to do freight. That's my job." She strode around to Gabby's desk and logged into the computer, pulling up the inventory screen. "I'll reprint all the labels with addresses and rerun the invoices. We can tape the new labels on top of the old ones, but you'll have to open all the envelopes to put the new invoices in."

I eyed the four freight totes lined up against the wall. My stomach got one of those disgusting feelings like I had eaten undercooked chicken. This was going to take way too much time to redo everything. I closed my eyes and tried to imagine a happy place—a beach somewhere where I was relaxing in the sun— and I forced myself to not cry as I waited for the new labels to print.

"Where is she anyway?" Sanita asked, while she took another slurp of her drink. Hearing only gurgles, it sounded like she didn't get anything out, but as if to tug on my nerves a little more, she went back in for another pull. This time an even louder slurp pulsated in the silence. I honestly couldn't understand how she could suck in all that air into such a short little body. Just when I had convinced myself that the noise was going to go on forever, she abruptly stopped.

I counted to three to avoid telling her that her drink was *obviously* empty, then I smiled as best as I could and said, "She had to meet with her model."

"Hmm." She thankfully tossed her empty noise maker in the trash, then grabbed the first sheet of new labels from the printer and handed them to me. "Just peel these off and stick them over the old ones."

"Thanks." I mournfully walked to the freight totes.

"I saw your commercial yesterday," she chatted after sliding her chair to the side to reload the printer with more labels. "You looked great."

"Thanks." Although it was extremely nice of her to compliment me, I wasn't in the mood for flattery and frankly, I felt so totally insecure in everything I had been doing, I didn't think I deserved a compliment. I dropped my first newly labeled envelope into a fresh new pile on the other side of the door and grabbed another envelope.

"Here . . ." I heard shuffling from her getting up from her chair and she continued to say, "I'll grab you a tote to put those in so they can stay organized." I kept my eyes down as I blazed through my pile, adamantly vowing to be done with my work detour by noon, determined to get a real lunch break today. She dropped a bin next to my foot. I restacked my pile inside it and worked conscientiously until a beep came from her phone, and she reported, "Gabby just texted me." I lifted my eyes ready to listen. "She's not going to get back for the giveaway drawing. She's wondering if you can do it without her."

I looked at the clock, which revealed we had ten minutes until the drawing. I didn't want to go on camera again, but I felt like I didn't have a choice. "I suppose I can, but can you work the camera?"

She was quiet while she finished texting, and then she raised her eyes again. "I can do that. I'll update the raffle app for you too if you want to get ready."

I blinked like I had woken up from a nap. After yesterday's marathon, I had totally dressed down today. Figuring I'd be doing freight all day, I had on a pair of mom jeans and a longer button-down shirt. I remembered Monica insisting on a quick hair brushing and fresh gloss before being recorded. So, I dug through my purse, searching for any little bit of makeup I might have had stashed. I was immediately grateful when I found sample sizes of powder I had gotten from the department store and hadn't had time to remove from my purse. I hurriedly concealed the red blotchy areas on my face and then moved on to groom my hair.

The thing with my hair is that it gets to a certain length and all it wants to do is look like a bush. It won't lay flat, and brushing almost always makes it worse, especially on humid days. I was overdue for a haircut and instantly regretted trying to brush it. I got frustrated and dug in my purse again for a hair tie, then I pulled the top half of my hair back into a messy bun. It wasn't perfect, but I knew it would have to be enough because it was getting too close to camera time. I crossed the floor to Gabby's desk to login to her website and get the camera on my phone set up. "So, how do you want to do this?" I waited for her to instruct me.

"You can be on camera, and I'll run the app when you say it's time. Then you can announce the winner. It should only take a few minutes."

"Sounds good." I drummed my fingers on the desk, waiting for the clock to tick away. "Let's go on now so we have time for people to join us before one."

"Good idea." She moved behind the desk in front of me.

I summoned my best Monica while she pressed record on my phone that she now pointed at me. "Hi, friends!" I smiled and waved into the camera. "This is Aubergine with Gabby Rue Fashion, and as promised we're going to draw a winner today. Remember, yesterday we opened the giveaway to anyone who bought a scarf from Gabby."

The people counter slowly ticked up, showing people were joining us. I waved again. "Welcome if you're just joining us. I'm going to get to this draw in a few minutes, but I do want to wait for a couple more people to hop on with us. So, I was talking about the giveaway. I have all the names of everyone who bought a scarf downloaded into an app that we will run in about two minutes. One lucky winner will receive a fashion makeover by Gabby."

I glanced at the people counter again. It hadn't moved, and my gut told me to stall a little longer. I motioned for Sanita to grab me a scarf from the pile resting in an opened tote. She wasted no time in grabbing one and handed it to me. I copied what Monica had done and wrapped it around my neck. "You can still get this gorgeous scarf if you want, but it's back ordered." Part of my hair bun must have fallen out because I felt a hair wisp against my face, and it was tickling behind my ear. I twitched my head to try to jerk my hair back, but it didn't work. Sanita started making an urgent motion with her hand, telling me to push my hair out of my face.

I did a casual hair toss, but I could still feel it. I looked on the computer screen to see if it was noticeable. Squinting my eyes for clear focus, I turned my head to see behind my ear, then I freaked! A cockroach must have crawled onto the scarf Sanita had given me, and when I wrapped it around my neck, it moved to my ear. I jolted off my chair. "It's on me! Get it off!"

Sanita's lips tightened downward and she put a finger up to her lips, trying to shush me while frantically pointing to the camera still recording. I don't know if I scared the bug with my screaming, but I now could feel it running down my neck and under my shirt collar. I panicked and waved my hands like I was drowning. "Get it off me!" I looked back and saw dozens more bugs on the floor again, all coming from the same hole in the wall as last night. Then it dawned on me that when Sanita gave me that bin, she took the bin that had been blocking the hole, unleashing the entire fleet again. *They were everywhere!* I instantly got overwhelmed and forgot the camera was on.

I tore at the back of my neck trying to get the creeper off me, but it was already under my shirt, and his little pokey legs ran further down my back. "Get it off me!" I screamed. I tried jumping up and down to make him fall to the floor, but his legs glue gripped. I tried reaching my back from every direction, but he was in the perfect middle spot where I couldn't reach. Then I saw the camera was recording and felt faint. "Shut the camera off!" I cried out to Sanita. The bug moved again, and I couldn't handle it. I was going to have to rip my shirt off, but I wasn't going to do that on camera! I ran to leave the room, but right before I got to the door, it flew open backwards at me and smacked me right in the face, knocking me out.

Chapter Five

"Her eyes are fluttering," Gabby's voice float above my face. "She's waking up." I was lying flat on the ground. I blinked my eyes opened to see Gabby standing over me. To the side of me, Sanita was fumigating the room with Gabby's spray and cussing in Spanish at the bugs when she scooped them into the trashcan. Gabby pushed a towel at me. "Here, put this on your head."

I touched my head where it throbbed, and my fingers warmed and moistened from fresh blood. I didn't have to ask why I needed the cloth and took it from her, pressing it to my cut. "How bad is it?" I tried to sit up because I was freaking out about being on the floor next to the bugs.

"You got a pretty big gash. Try to hold pressure on it for a few minutes and then I'll look again."

I surveyed my space bubble for roaches and thankfully didn't see any, so I let my head relax back down on the ground. Sanita had resorted to ninja stomping on the roaches that refused to die from the spray. Then I remembered the camera. "Did you shut the camera off?"

"I did . . ." Gabby started, "but not before everyone got a show. It's okay though. Glad you're okay."

"Did I run into the door?"

"I hit you with it. I came back to help with the drawing. I heard screaming in here, so I ran down the hall and rushed through the door. I had no idea you'd be standing right there." She made a squeamish smile and added, "Sorry."

"It's okay." I slowly stretched my neck to the side to see if it was sore. Then I peeled the cloth away from my face. "How does it look now?" I could feel the blood starting to ooze already.

She barely looked at it before her lips bent down. "You better put that towel back on it. You're going to need stitches." She stood and retrieved her phone. "I'll call for a cab. You stay lying down."

I pressed the cloth to my head and stared at the ceiling, but in an unsettling way, it made me dizzy. After she had requested my ride, I asked her, "Did you do the draw?"

She hovered over me; empathy was deep in her eyes. "You don't need to worry about that now. Just relax. I'll do it later. I'll have to do a video later to explain what happened anyway."

Starting to feel a tad nauseous, I let my lids drift closed. I was about to fall into a light sleep when I heard Gabby say, "Your cab's here. Do you have someone you want me to call to help you?"

I visualized Fulton's face as he heard that, once again, he would need to come to my rescue. He would be there for me too, but something made me want to do this on my own. "I'll be okay."

"Then I'll send Sanita with you," Gabby insisted. "She's good at bossing people around. She'll take care of you."

"Okay," I agreed a little breathlessly. I was relieved to have help going to the clinic, but I was also relieved to be done working. I tried to tell myself that it was normal to feel that about a new job, reassuring myself that my days here would get better, but as I got up and continued to press the cloth on my face to avoid bleeding out, I had my doubts.

"Your video went viral," Gabby reported over the phone the next day.

I inched myself to the edge of my bed like I was expecting an ambush, terrified of what day three of working with Gabby would bring. "What?" My short-term memory was fogged from the minor concussion I'd suffered.

"Sorry."

"For what?" I dropped my feet over the edge of my bed and felt like I was about to get into a tank of sharks.

"Your video. I tried to get it deleted but it was too late. It went viral. There's even people who created memes of it dubbing it 'the roach dance.'"

"Hmm."

"I'd stay offline for a couple days if I were you."

"That shouldn't be a problem since I never really got back online from living out West," I said. In the back of my head, I could see Becky and Tina watching my video and laughing their faces off, but other than them, I didn't really know anyone anyways. At this point there was nothing I could do about it, so I decided to let go of my embarrassment.

"Does your head hurt?" Gabby asked.

"It does. It's sore where the gash is, and I have a massive headache." I raised myself to my feet, making my way to my closet.

"You don't have to come in today."

"It's okay. I can make it. I might need something to do to keep my mind off it."

"Please, I'd feel better if you take the day off." Her voice was soft and genuine, so I accepted.

"Okay. I guess so . . ."

"If it's any consolation, my website has been slammed with sales. Apparently, memes are good for publicity. I've honestly doubled my sales for the whole year since you've been here."

"You don't need help with freight?" I double-checked.

"Sanita got all the scarves we had in inventory packaged last night, so we're waiting for more of those."

"So, you don't need me to do anything then?" I confirmed again. I heard her talking, but my head pulsated so severely I couldn't really comprehend what she had said.

"I don't want to say you're not needed, because you're always welcome to come in, but I really insist you take the day off."

I looked down at my feet, and the backs of my heels were still rubbed raw from Monday. "Alright," I agreed as she didn't have to tell me twice. I needed to clear my head in more than one way. We ended our call, and I spent the day drifting in and out of a light sleep. Good rest wasn't really an option since my head hurt so badly, but I made no effort to get anything productive done.

However, I appreciated the time off and told myself this job had to get better now.

That evening, I tucked my head under an umbrella, grateful for the misting rain as it gave me a way to hide my face even more in the night shadows. I slowed as I reached the theatre and browsed the winding line outside.

"Over here." Fulton waved from his spot near the front of the line.

My shoulders relaxed when his eyes met mine. "Can I cut in next to you?" I asked him.

He scooted back. "Sure, stand in front of me." I entered the line, but it was super squished with people so I had to stand so ultra-close to him, that I could smell his aftershave, or wait, he didn't look like he had just shaved, maybe it was his deodorant? Whatever it was, it was definitely one of those scents that just kept reminding me of how close we were. I searched my brain for words to start a conversation, but I could feel his eyes on my head bandage. "How are you feeling?" he asked.

"Like I had a concussion."

"You should've said something. It probably wasn't a good idea to walk here tonight."

"It was fine. I actually think the fresh air is the only thing that's helped all day."

His eyebrows furrowed but before he could speak, a blonde female squeezed in between the two of us which was pretty much impossible since we barely had a slice of air between us. I don't know how she did it but after she had transplanted, she flung her long blonde hair over her shoulder, looked at Fulton. "Fulton, are you going to introduce me to your friend?"

He motioned to me with his head. "Yeah, this is Abs." Then he turned back toward the woman and said, "This is Candace."

I recognized her from the day I had visited Fulton in his dorm room last year. She had one of those faces that was unforgettable because she looked like she had won the beauty gene pool in every category. Her face turned to stare at me, but she continued to speak to Fulton, "Oh, this is your *high-school* friend."

I blinked like I was trying to digest a punch. Fulton obviously didn't hear her insult because he just flashed his easy grin at me. "Yep, this is her."

"We've all seen your video." She reached under my umbrella and touched below my bandage. "That was tragic. Are you feeling better?"

I froze, feeling violated from her touch. I didn't feel any better. I didn't even want to come here tonight, but Fulton had practically begged me to meet him here. Even my dad called and told me he wanted me to get out of the house and thought it was a good idea to do something to make me laugh. I couldn't tell her the truth though. "I'm alright."

"Good. I hope it heals for you. I wouldn't want you to have a scar on your pretty face." The way she said *pretty* sounded like she was talking to a child, and not only did it not feel genuine, but it was also annoying. I watched Fulton to see if he was crowded by her trying to smash in between us, but he seemed comfortable.

The doors opened and the line started to move forward. Fulton leaned closer to me, trying to speak above the crowd noise. "Wally saves us a table upfront, but it comes with a price."

I moved up a couple of spaces in line, then recentered my gaze back on him. "What's that?"

"You know how comedians like to pick on their audience, right?"

"Sure."

"He usually does a pretty good job at humiliating us all. I wanted to warn you."

"Okay . . ." I brushed his comment away without even thinking about it because I was used to him being sort of a paranoid-overthinker. I watched for the couple in front of me to finish paying, and I pulled my wallet out of my purse.

"Don't worry about it." Fulton waved my wallet away. "Wally gave me some promotional tickets." He produced three tickets out of his wallet and handed them to the usher. He pointed to me and Candace. "For us three," he told the usher.

I folded my umbrella, hooking it on the strap of my cross-body purse. We passed through the door with Candace superglued to Fulton's hip. I was relieved when she announced she needed to use the restroom before we went inside. "Is she, like, your girlfriend?" I blurted out after the bathroom door closed behind her.

His eyes flashed empathy at me, or maybe it was confusion. "Nah . . . we're good friends."

"Hmm." It didn't matter what he said about her, I definitely started to feel out of place, like a third wheel. It was embarrassing enough to be here in public looking like a mummy, but I didn't need to feel like I was the tag along. If I tried to leave, Fulton wouldn't let me and it would cause a bigger scene, so I stewed and wished the night was over already.

He must've picked up on my uneasy feelings because he added, "We have a lot of classes together. She's a super nice girl."

Nice. That's exactly why she was here. She was a nice girl. That's what Fulton liked. I immediately remembered how Fulton had thought I was a mean girl. Then Candace strolled out of the bathroom and reattached herself to Fulton's hip. I let myself fall behind their perfectly aligned steps as we walked to our table. A sickness crept inside the pit of my stomach. We got closer to our table where a few of Wally's friends were already sitting. Fulton seemed like he was about to sit, but instead he glanced back at me with a look of apology.

"What?"

His brows were wrinkled like he was worried about something as he pointed to the chair next to him. "You can sit here."

"Okay." I moved over to the chair he was offering and didn't waste a moment to slump down into it, but Fulton still stood stiffly next to me. So, I raised my face to be able to look back at him and asked, "What's wrong?"

"I hope you have a good sense of humor tonight."

"Why?"

"You'll find out in a minute."

I lowered my body even further in my chair and pondered the odd warning. *Of course I had a good sense of humor.* I could be a lot of fun when I wanted. How dare he think I didn't like a comedy show.

Chapter Six

I tensely tapped my foot on the floor, feeling left out. More people sat at our table, but I didn't really know how to join in their conversations. Every time Fulton tried to start a conversation with me, Candace would lean over and start blabbing about herself again, and that would pull his attention back to her. I was relieved when the lights dimmed, and I didn't have to pretend not to feel ignored anymore.

I shifted my gaze to side stage where there was movement, and my bottom jaw dropped into a gasp. Wally had strutted out wearing a full-size cockroach costume complete with a headpiece with stuffed antennas creepily planted on the top of his head. When he stopped at center stage, Fulton's eye's shot toward me and I felt my cheeks glow. "I didn't know," he mouthed to me.

Wally's words telling me to be a fun girl echoed in my head. "It's okay," I mouthed back.

Wally spoke into the microphone using a character voice he had created; it was deep, measured, and sounded slightly Italian. "I have a problem." He looked out at the crowd with a worried expression. "I'm feeling misunderstood because everyone thinks I was trying to be scary. I don't like to scare people. You see, my name is Raymond, and I'm a romantic roach." His facial expression timed perfectly with his comedic pause.

I buried my face into my palm, as I knew exactly where this skit was going. Fulton offered a sympathetic look. I faintly heard Raymond explain how he was on my ear because he was only trying to talk to me, but he had become intoxicated from the smell of my hair, which made him disoriented, thus causing him to wander.

I hardly listened to the skit at this point because it was actually more intriguing to watch Fulton, who had an expression on his face I didn't recognize. His lips were firm and pressed together and his gaze was hyper-focused on Wally. I was able to laugh more at Wally's jokes than he was, and I even caught him shushing Candace once when she tried talking to him.

Wally continued his skit, interacting with the audience very naturally with his new character. When it was over, he exited the stage; the audience clapped for several minutes, and the next comedian came out. As soon as it was quieter, Fulton leaned over and in a hushed voice said, "He had asked me if I thought you could take a joke. That's why I warned you outside, but I had no idea he had this planned."

"It's okay. It was fun."

His eyebrow arched. "Fun? I thought it seemed sort of juvenile. You liked it?"

"I probably would have liked it better if it weren't true, but he was funny." I was proud of myself for not getting offended too easily. The old Abs wouldn't have been able to be the butt of a joke like this. I could dish it out all the time, but I would never have been able to receive it. But after I got over the initial shock, and I was able to listen to Wally's jokes, he was funny. I enjoyed being able to laugh as it had been ages.

After the show, we gathered on the sidewalk outside. Exhausted from my week, I wanted to leave but I could feel Fulton watching me. I could tell he wanted to talk. Thankfully, Candace's micro dress must have been squeezing her bladder because she excused herself again, and Fulton didn't waste a moment to pull me aside. "Are you sure that didn't bother you?"

"Nah, he was funny. I actually laughed a ton." I struggled to open my umbrella, but I finally got it up on the third try. Then I held it above both of our heads. He was quiet for longer than what should have been comfortable. Finally, he said, "I guess I didn't realize."

"Realize what?"

"I think it's weird that he would single you out like that. He barely knows you."

I shrugged, getting a little shiver from the dampness in the air. "According to what Gabby told me, everyone knows me now thanks to my roach dance." I spotted Candace walking out of the building, heading to our group. Her eyes were moving fast, more than likely scanning for Fulton. We only had a couple seconds before Candace would laser in on him which made me sad because this night had been nothing like I had thought it would be. I had envisioned Fulton and I actually talking more than just pleasantries. Tipping my head towards him, I softly said, "Thanks for inviting me,"

"I'm glad you came. Sorry I didn't get to talk to you much. I guess I didn't think it would be so crazy with everyone here."

His serious expression made me miss our old midnight chats at the farm where it was just the two of us. And if I wasn't already befuddled enough after Fulton had told me that he had missed me the other night, he now added to the confusion, by leaning in slightly—even more than would be needed to share the same umbrella— and saying in a private voice, "We'll have to make plans to have dinner just the two of us." I'm pretty sure my lips fell completely agape, thinking Fulton was asking me on a real date but then he quickly added, "so we can catch up."

"Oh, yeah... to catch up." I closed my mouth, feeling like a fool. "I'd like that."

"Fulton," Candace called from in front of an opened car door. "My ride share is here, and we have room for one more."

Fulton looked at her and called, "Go ahead, I should walk Abs home. It's sort of late—"

"Go ahead, I can walk her back," Wally cut in from where he appeared near the theatre exit.

Fulton's gaze bounced from Wally and then to Candace, who was still standing on the street, waiting for him. "I can walk myself. It's only a few blocks," I said, starting to feel uncomfortable for Fulton.

"Nah, I'm happy to walk you," Wally insisted. "I'm always a little hyper when I get off stage, so I need to burn off some energy. And Fulton—" he turned towards him "—you have an eight o'clock class, so you should go ahead and take the ride. I don't have class until eleven, if I even go."

Fulton's lips were tight as he listened to Wally, then he turned toward me. "What do you think?"

"I'm fine, really. You guys can both go."

"There's only room for one," Wally said.

"Are you coming?" Candace called again, standing with one hand now on her hip.

Fulton's eyes bounced from the car to me. "I do have an early class, and I need to study tonight too, so if it's okay, I'll take the ride."

"Sure." I waved toward the car. "Go home. Study."

"Okay," he said, then added briskly, "I'll text you tomorrow about our plans to get together."

"Sure," I said. His eyes lingered on mine for a tiny second. If I would have known better, I would have thought he was upset, but he didn't hold it long enough for me to question it before he turned and sprinted to the car.

Feeling so totally confused by what had just happened with Fulton, I turned to Wally. I let out a deep breath and then said, "You really don't need to walk me home. It's only a few blocks."

"It's cool." He nodded his head toward the sidewalk, inviting me to start walking. "I feel like I owe you restitution."

My lips curled and I insisted, "I'm not mad."

"I'm impressed you didn't throw something at me."

I stole a quick glance at him as we fell into a steady stride toward my street. "Nah, do people really throw things at you?"

"Sure. Not as much as they used to, but it happens."

Feeling good about how easily we were able to fall into small talk, I continued with the topic and asked, "What's something someone threw at you?"

"Well, at one of the first shows I ever did, there was this little blue-haired lady sitting in the front row. I assumed people knew that if you sit in front, you're going to get picked on, but she didn't laugh or even smile at any of my jokes. I should've left her alone, but I made a joke about how her denture cream must have slipped and glued her lips shut."

"How'd that go over?"

"She didn't do anything right away, so I thought maybe she was deaf and didn't hear my jokes. After the show, I was standing out by the concessions, and she threw her leftover drink at me."

I let my hand cover my mouth. "No way."

"She did. I learned from that experience that if someone isn't laughing or smiling, I shouldn't pick on them because they aren't going to have a sense of humor about it."

"That seems backwards. Most of the comedians I've seen love to pick on the people who don't laugh."

"Most do," he said, looking over at me briefly, "but that's not my style. I don't want to make fun of people. I want to make them feel good."

"Well, you were pretty funny," I affirmed.

"Thanks. So, what kinds of things are you doing at Gabby's?" We turned the corner onto my avenue and into the wind. I adjusted the umbrella, turning my head to shield my face from the rain that drifted under the canopy. I got to see the side of his face perfectly, and he looked genuinely interested, waiting to hear my response.

"It's only been a couple of days, so I'm not sure yet. Next week is fashion week, and it makes everything busier than normal. So far, I've mostly done sales and freight."

"Do you think you'll like it?"

"It's okay. Better than living off-grid."

"Fulton told me a few crazy stories from your life back there. He said one time you got chased by a bear?"

"Yeah." I took a large step over a puddle. "Good thing you didn't see that, or you would have had to do a bear dance skit tonight." I looked at him sideways and caught the end of his lips curving up.

"I don't think a romantic bear would be as humorous as a romantic roach."

"Probably not." Motioning to my nearing doorstep, I announced, "We're here." Then I halted my steps, turning to face him. "Are you walking back to campus?"

"Yeah, I love walking, especially at night. I get to people watch, and I make up stories about what their lives are like. It gives me content for my shows."

I reached my umbrella forward. "Then keep this."

"Are you sure?"

"Yeah, it's supposed to pick up after midnight, so you might get stuck in a downpour. You'll need it."

"Okay, I'll hurry back then." With a brief pause, he flashed me one more smile, and then said, "Thanks."

"You're welcome. Thanks for walking me home." I turned to enter the building, and I realized I was in a good mood that actually remained even after I thought about going back to work tomorrow. *It has to get better from here, I told myself.*

Chapter Seven

"Look at this clown," Gabby's disgruntled mutter spewed out as soon as I passed through the door the next morning.

I did my now traditional scan of the floor, looking for roaches. When I was convinced there were none, I slowly tiptoed to my chair while staying on guard and stowed my purse under my neatly organized desk. "What's going on?"

Her blue eyes—slightly more fiery than usual—fixed on me. "Have you seen any of the memes or anything out there about your roach dance?"

I plopped down to sit, rotating my chair to face her. "Nope, I've completely avoided the internet."

Her barely-there eyebrows knitted together. "Well, I thought maybe it would be old news today, but there's this comedian who created a whole character out of that cockroach. He performed it in a theatre last night and, of course, it's all over social media today."

I sucked my lip in hard, holding it there. I didn't know if I should confess that I knew who he was and that I had gone out last night and saw it, especially since I technically skipped work yesterday, but I figured honesty was going to be the best option. "I know him," I blurted out before she could expand. "He's a roommate to my friend."

She tapped her finger on her screen with the video loaded. "You know him?"

"Not real well."

"So, you saw this?" She looked back at me, eyes narrowed into an inquiring look. I gave a shallow nod, not wanting to elaborate on the fact I had been there. My answer must have satisfied her because she lowered her gaze and said, "Okay then. If it doesn't bother you, we don't need to dwell on it." Then she retrieved her clipboard, and reached her petite arm long across her desk, handing it to me. "Here's the information for the giveaway winner. She's going to be stopping in sometime this morning, but I have to go meet my seamstress about fashion week stuff, so could you do her measurements and interview her to see what styles she likes so I get an idea of what dress to give her?"

I read the information, and it seemed simple enough. "Sure, I can take a couple of pictures too so you can see her overall look, if that helps."

"That would be great." She rolled her chair back and stood up with the speed of my grandma which seemed odd since she was usually always running at top speed. I continued to watch her with a cautious eye until she yawned and said, "Actually, since you're here, I might zip out now because I want to grab some breakfast before my meeting."

"That's fine." I tapped the stack of invoices in the basket. "Do you want me to work on freight until she comes?"

"Yes, please do." She flung her bag over her shoulder and added, "That should keep you more than busy."

I got to work, organizing my freight station, clearing away the clutter that was left by the last person who had used it—prolly Sanita. I resisted rolling my eyes because she obviously wasn't concerned about leaving the station tidy for me, but I had quickly learned I didn't like working in a mess and it was worth it to me to clean first. Then Gabby breezed right by me and out the door before I had time to tell her bye. I brushed away the last of the garbage, when my fingers touched against something sticky. This time I rolled my eyes as hard as I could. It was a ring stain obviously from Sanita's old drink cup that she carelessly never wiped up. "I don't know what I'm going to do about her," I muttered under my breath as I reached for the surface cleaner and spritz my countertop. I had just started to wipe it dry, when my phone rang. I leaned over, peeking into my opened purse and saw Fulton's name glowing on my phone screen. Without wasting a moment, I eagerly answered, "Hey."

"How's it going?"

"It's good. You're up early."

"Yeah, I had my eight o'clock class this morning. We had a test, and we got to leave when we finished it, so I'm done already."

"Everything alright?" I asked.

"Yeah, why?"

"It's just that you never call."

"Well, I'm walking to my next class and it's easier to talk when I walk."

"Oh." I put my phone on speaker and set it down. I picked up my first invoice, studying it as I walked to the clothing racks in the back of the studio to locate the items to fulfill the order. "So, what's up?"

"I told you that I'd call to make plans to get together. I was wondering how tonight works for you?"

I flipped through hangers looking for a navy V-neck wool sweater to match the description on my invoice. "Tonight?"

"Do you have any plans?"

"Not really." I paused because I found a matching sweater and checked the SKU. "Found it."

"Huh?"

"Oh, I'm sorry. I'm trying to pull freight for orders, and I have no idea what I'm doing." I flipped to the next sweater to find one in a medium size. "I have no idea what time I get done with work, but I would probably be free to do something," I said, then added, "Maybe grab a bite to eat." I found my sweater, pulled it from the rack and set my sights on the next item on the invoice.

"Okay, how about you text me when you get off?"

"Deal." I flashed a winning grin when I easily found the white tank I needed.

"Okay, I'll let you get back to work then."

"Okay, bye." I ended the call and continued to fill orders until the giveaway winner arrived. I had just wrapped up my meeting with her and was about to step out for lunch when Gabby returned with a scowl on her face. She was clearly trying to avoid eye contact with me.

"I got all my invoices done," I reported. "You had a lot of orders for those mom jean capris with red stitching."

"Yeah," she answered robotically as she frantically typed into her computer search screen.

"And the winner came," I said, continuing to fill her in about my morning. "She was super excited. I got her file done." I grabbed the clipboard off my desk and tried giving it to Gabby, but she ignored me. So I slid it onto the corner of her desk, I asked softly, "Are you mad at me?"

She placed her hand on her forehead like she was dizzy. "I'm sorry. What?"

"How did your meeting go?"

"It went fine until I got a message from my building manager."

"Did he finally get back to you about the roaches?" I asked.

"No. He's evicting me."

My eyebrows arched in red alert. "What? I thought you paid your rent."

"I did. Barely. But it wasn't about that. He's been inundated with complaints from concerned citizens about the building and the roaches. The Chinese restaurant below has lost all their business and are trying to file a lawsuit. The comedian clown friend of yours set off another spiral of too much attention. It's a mess."

My feet fumbled backwards in small steps when I understood she might be blaming me for this. "Can he evict you for that?"

"I don't know. I could call my lawyer, but I'm swamped with fashion week starting tomorrow and my business blowing up in sales." She must have reminded herself to check her orders because she went to the sales screen and refreshed it. "Look, another hundred and some orders just this hour." She selected the print option, and the printer beeped and shifted to life.

"That's a good thing, right?" I squeaked out in a tiny reassuring voice.

"It is, but the timing's terrible. Apparently, your friend is good for my business but bad for everyone else."

I swallowed, feeling my throat drying up as my anxiety flowed in. "I'm sorry. I had no idea he was going to do that."

She let out a sigh, not like she was overly upset, but more just overwhelmed. "It's okay, everyone else is making fun of it too, but I guess he was sort of the last straw."

"So now what are you going to do?" I wanted to appear industrious, so I immediately grabbed the invoices that she had printed, and I returned to my freight station to work, feeling guilty with my ears attuned.

She buried her face in her hands to stifle a scream. When she came up for oxygen, she looked surprisingly calm like screaming had helped. "I'm going to call a realtor and get something lined up ASAP. I'm not even going to fight this slumlord. I think it'll be a blessing in the end because it's such a dump, but I couldn't afford anything else when I signed this lease. Now business is better, so I'm hoping to get something nicer."

I trapped my air in my chest waiting for her to scold me.

She continued, "Plus, I've had to ramp up production, and those new orders are coming in from manufacturing starting in a month and I won't have the place to store them here. I'm launching my Gold Couture line next week, and that freight is supposed to start arriving tomorrow so I can be ready for orders after our show. I was going to rent the storage loft above me for that—" she pointed toward the ceiling— "but now with the roaches and the eviction, I'm not pursuing that anymore." She placed her hand firmly on the desk and scanned the studio. "We are out of space. I need something bigger."

"What do you need me to do to make this easier for you?" I peeped out, terrified of what she would say.

"Well, I had lined up Sanita to come in all day tomorrow and all next week for freight, so you can let that freight sit. I've been asked to contribute a body to help with setting up chairs for fashion week in Bryant Park." Her eyebrows arched in my direction. "Could you run over there and see what you can help with?"

"Sure." I willingly set the pants I was holding on the freight table. "You want me to leave now?"

"Yeah, that'll be good. You can walk over there and do what they need you to do. Make sure you sign in. Then come back here in the morning and, hopefully, I'll be a little more organized."

"Absolutely, I can do that." I quickly cleaned my freight table to look orderly, knowing it wouldn't be that way when I returned. I told myself that maybe when Sanita saw how clean I kept my space, she would eventually take a hint and clean up her mess. "Do you need me to be early tomorrow?" I asked, while I crossed the floor.

"Can you be here by six?" Her eyes were already focused on a realtor website.

"I'd be happy to," I said. Then I left feeling guilty but thankful that I got to give Gabby some space while she worked through her new obstacle that *unfortunately* I had been the cause of.

Chapter Eight

Battling the overhead autumn sun, while setting up chairs in Bryant Park, I managed to bite my tongue from all the sarcasms wanting to spring out of my mouth until it was five. Without wasting another second, I ducked out before anyone spotted me leaving and I immediately dialed Fulton. "Hey, I'm getting off work, and I'm starving. Ready to eat?"

"Ug, I'm so sorry, I forgot when I asked you that I was on the volunteer schedule at the vet clinic tonight."

My shoulders drooped in disappointment. "Oh, okay—"

"—I still want to see you," he quickly cut in, "but I need to get my chores done. Do you want to meet me there? If you help, it'll go faster."

"That depends . . ." I adjusted my purse on my tired shoulder. I had just got done working an eight-hour shift, and I was cautious about agreeing to more free labor.

"On what?"

"What do you do there?"

"It's easy. I mostly clean cages."

"You scoop the poop?" I asked, unamused as his invitation to hang out just kept getting less glamorous.

"Yep, just like on the farm."

"Well, you should be awesome at that," I teased.

"I don't want to brag, but I am a bit of an expert. Would you want to help?"

I sighed deeply, wanting to go home to throw my feet up and do nothing, but the familiar sound of his voice had me instantly reminiscing about our days of camaraderie on the ranch—my heart twisted gently, urging me. Before I knew it, I was completely lured in. "Sure, I can meet you there. Text me the address." I hung up my phone, waiting for his text which only took a second, providing me with an address, that I quickly noticed was only a few blocks from where I was, so I briskly walked until I found the brick building with the vet logo. Not stopping for even a breath, I went inside and was greeted by a receptionist.

"Hi, I'm meeting a friend to help volunteer—"

"Back here." Fulton stuck his head out from the hall and said, "Come on back."

"Hey." I passed through the hall and into the back room that consisted of cement floors with two large pens on one side and stacks of different sized wire kennels on the other side. The odor reeked more of wet dog than it did of fresh pooh, so I wasn't overly grossed out, but it still took me a moment to adjust my senses.

"They weren't that busy today, so we just need to clean the pens and the kennels on the top row. Then we're good." He pointed to a small cleaning cart. "Do you want to grab some gloves and collect the pee pads?"

I let my tongue roll over the front of my teeth, moistening my mouth so I could handle the smells without gagging, and sarcastically replied, "That sounds glamorous. I'd love to." I pulled a latex glove from the box and stretched it as I pushed my hand inside, letting the end of the glove snap back dramatically like I saw them do on T.V.

"Sorry, I know this is gross. But it looks good on vet school applications." He flung the door of one of the large pens opened, and a rust-colored dog who looked identical to a bear cub slowly moved right into Fulton's opened arms to receive a hug and head scratching. "This is Pumpkin," Fulton explained, his eyes lighting up in the same manner that reminded me of a child who sees their favorite toy. Obviously, Fulton wasn't a child or even childlike, but the joy he felt from being with animals was something that overflowed, and I found myself feeling honored to be able to see him in his element. Fulton scratched behind Pumpkin's ears, triggering his black tongue to hang out from his giant contagious smile. Fulton explained, "He's mostly blind and deaf, but he knows me because I've been feeding him for the last year."

"He's blind and deaf? Poor dog." My feet shuffled forward to pet him but stopped when I heard a warning growl.

"He's pretty cautious around new people. I'd stay back," Fulton warned. "Chows can be mean if they feel threatened."

I planted my feet, now afraid to move forward. "How'd he become blind and deaf?"

"Chows have problems with their eyes. It's a breed thing, but it usually isn't this bad. He showed signs of abuse when he was picked up by animal patrol last year. The pound was going to euthanize him since he overstayed his allotted time, but the vet here decided to take him in. He's a vet pet and lives here full time."

"That's so sad." I watched Pumpkin rub the side of his head next to Fulton's cheek. Then added, "It's so cute how he trusts you."

"We're buds." Fulton patted Pumpkin's side and then stood up and moved to start cleaning.

I followed his lead, opening the first dirty kennel, removed the potty pad and dumped it in the trash. "You're the only person I'd scoop poop for," I declared with more humor that I actually felt.

His perfect teeth flashed when his lips curled up. "I'd have to agree. I don't know any other girls who would scoop poop with me."

"Candace would." I regretted saying it as soon as I blurted it out.

"Nah, she wouldn't." After a short pause, he continued in a low, more thoughtful tone, "I was going to bring her up but didn't know how."

My spine stiffened but I opened the next kennel and fished out the soiled pad, trying to pretend to be neutral to any comment about her. "Oh," was the only reply I could muster up.

He scooped food from a bin into Pumpkin's bowl, keeping his head low, while talking, "I'm not sure what got into her last night. She's never like that. I'm not sure how it looked to you, but if you couldn't tell, I was having a hard time with her clinginess."

I grabbed the disinfectant spray and spritzed the kennels I had emptied. "I didn't notice."

Without looking in my direction, he walked back to the pen with the full bowl. I could see the unsettlement in his eyes when he said, "I actually think she was jealous of you, which blows my mind because she has nothing to be jealous of you about."

I wiped off the excess cleaner with a dry paper towel and tried to hold my tongue. It felt like he'd just given me a massive insult even though I knew he was more thinking out loud about what happened than trying to understand how he was making me feel. Candace's ears must have been ringing because Fulton's phone beeped. He glanced at it and said, "It's her." He paused as he read her text and it was so quiet, I forced myself to whistle to drown out the silence, while I added clean potty pads to each kennel. Pumpkin had laid back down in his kennel next to his dish of newly replenished food. I kept my distance from the pup, but we both watched Fulton spend at least five minutes constructing a response text. "Problems?" I asked when he finally looked up from his screen.

"Uh, no. Sorry about that. She was wondering what lotto numbers I picked for class." He grabbed a broom from the cleaning cart and started to sweep out the other large kennel.

I leaned against the wall, waiting since my kennels were cleaned. "Are you taking Lotto 101?"

"No, it's actually for our statistics class. Our professor gave us an assignment to pick lottery numbers for this week's drawing using probability of numbers based on the numbers that have been recently used."

"Sounds like he's trying to get rich from your work."

"Nah, he likes to make things practical. Plus, he's one of those people who actually thinks math is fun."

"So, are you going to buy a lottery ticket?"

"Yeah, that's what we were texting about. I gave her my numbers, and she's going to get our tickets just for fun." He hooked the broom back onto the cleaning cart and shut the pen door. "I think we're done in here."

"Looks good to me." I tucked my lip in, wondering if maybe I should cut out now because I really didn't want to spend the next hour talking about Candace, but my stomach quietly reminded me that I was still hungry, so I decided to stick with the plan and asked, "Ready to go eat?"

"Yeah, let's go before the dinner rush."

I removed my gloves and scrubbed my hands in the sink by the door and waited for Fulton to do the same. While he scrubbed, he explained, "There's a great Mexican take-out place around the corner . . . or do you want something more American?"

I folded my arms across my chest, still unimpressed by how this conversation was going. "Mexican sounds good." He was silent as he yanked out a paper towel, and hurriedly dried his hands, tossed the towel in the trash, and headed toward the door. I struggled to follow him, wondering what the rush was, but I stayed right by his side, as he stepped onto the sidewalk and took a left. "That'll be good and quick too," he said when he finally broke his own silence.

I checked my watch, noting it was a little past six. "Are you in a hurry?"

"Not a real big hurry, but I always have studying to do."

My enthusiasm about spending time with Fulton had mostly dissipated by now because he seemed so distracted compared to when we used to hang out together on the farm. I understood he was busy, but I was busy too. I wondered if he was hanging out with me out of a feeling of obligation based on something my dad asked him to do. I knew my dad and he would definitely ask Fulton to keep tabs on me. I didn't want to believe that's why he invited me out, but I was starting to get suspicious. "Well, I don't have to take up your time, if you have other stuff you need to do," I said.

"Oh no." A line creased in his brow. Then his eyes flicked over to meet mine, but for the first time all night, I could see him really focus on me. "That came out wrong. I want to see you. But I'm sure you know how it is; there's always stuff you should be doing. I'm sure you're swamped with work too."

"Yeah," I agreed deciding to let him off the hook for being distracted. I eagerly changed the subject away from poop and Candace. "It's way crazier than I could have ever imagined, especially for the first week. Each day keeps getting busier."

"What kind of stuff does she have you doing?"

"Besides battling roaches?"

"Yeah, besides that." He smirked, finding time to reconnect our eyes again and I sort of melted—feeling like he was really trying to understand something about my life.

"Well, today I had to set up for fashion week, which wouldn't have been bad, but it was smoldering hot out. My head wound was literally pulsing."

"That doesn't sound good." His gaze traced my bandage, but instead of making me insecure, it affirmed my feelings that he was concerned about me. Then he added, "Gabby should let you rest for a few days."

"I think she would, but she needs help. She's busy with sales and has no staff, plus today she found out she got evicted—thanks to Wally's little performance last night—so I really felt bad."

His already concerned brow creased even deeper. "How did Wally get her evicted?"

"It's a long story but basically the building manager got annoyed from all the negative attention the roach skit gave him. I think Wally pushed him over the edge. So, now we must move, and we have only a few weeks to find a place. Her job is so high stress, I honestly don't know how she does it."

Fulton crossed to the inside of the sidewalk to a brightly painted door and opened it for me. "It's right in here." The smell of chilies and beer wafted under my nose as we moved to the counter to order. "They have the best guacamole," Fulton said from behind me, waiting for me to read the menu. He flashed his debit card at me. "And it's my treat."

"Sweet, thanks." I looked at the person behind the counter. "I'll have the taco platter with chicken, please."

"I'll have the burrito plate with extra guac, and no onions," Fulton ordered, waited for the total, and swiped his card. He grabbed our plastic drink cups, and we filled them, then slid into a booth to wait for our number to be called. Fulton casually leaned over across the table and picked up our conversation. "Well, now I feel responsible for your eviction since I'm the one who introduced you to Wally."

I swallowed my first sip of some weird cherry-flavored drink I had selected from the fountain. "Nah, it's not your fault any more than it was mine, or Wally's or Gabby's. It's how it worked out."

"It stinks, though, because it sort of reflects on you."

"She wasn't mad at me."

"That's good, I guess. But I still feel like I should try to help you. If you need help with the move, let me know. I can round up a few buddies to help too."

"That might be nice. I'll let you know if we need you once I know what Gabby plans."

Our number was called and Fulton got up and grabbed our tray of food and brought it back to the table. I retrieved my plate, picked up my taco and eagerly bit into it. After a few moments of silent chewing, his phone beeped. He read his text, then looked back at me. "Sorry, I'm going to reply fast and then I'll put my phone away." I didn't care anymore that Candace had him on such a short leash. I was famished and my taco was a saucy mess of delectable goodness. I stuffed my face while he checked in with her again. Then when he finally set his phone screen down on the table, he announced, "I'm done."

Not wanting to talk about Candace anymore, I asked, "Isn't it crazy how fast you got used to having a phone all the time again?"

He nodded as he chewed and then swallowed. "Yeah, it's hard to even remember Montana anymore. Life moves so fast and I'm so busy with my classes, it feels like it was a hundred years ago."

I felt melancholy because I could remember perfectly what happened in Montana and how we had become allies. I blinked away his comment because it felt like it had plucked a fullness from my heart that I had gained from being his friend. I quickly asked another question to avoid getting sad. "So, what other classes are you taking?"

"I have an overload this semester because I wanted to finish all my sciences this year so I can apply for better internships this summer."

I had finished my plate of food, and I leaned back against the booth, watching him eat. "That sounds like a lot of hard classes."

"It is, but hopefully it pays off. If I can get a good internship, it'll help me get into vet school. It's disheartening how selective they are. It's actually easier to get into medical school."

"Maybe med school can be your back-up plan?"

"I don't even want to think about this not working out. It's all I think about anymore. I love it so much."

"I love how you've jumped in headfirst."

He lowered his taco back to his plate, while he looked back at me with a puzzled look on his face. "What do you mean?"

"You are working so hard, but I could tell by the way you looked at Pumpkin that you got more from him than he could ever get from you." His eyes flickered with a sensitivity I used to see when he cared for animals on the farm. It was relieving to me in a weird way to see that expression, like maybe it was evidence that he still was a little of who he was then. Then I added, "Not that you're not great with him or helpful to him, but I can tell it means a lot to you to be able to care for him."

"I never thought about it like that, but I'd agree with you." His lips stretched into a satisfied smile, tipping his brow just a slight measure toward me. It was an innocent enough gesture but when he lifted his eyes, they hit me in this crazy, insane bullseye of a target that I didn't even know was attached to my heart. *There was that look again.* "I appreciate you saying that."

"You're welcome." Then all the sudden out of nowhere my fired on. It was super awkward, so I blurted out a random comment, "And thanks for letting me see you do what you do best."

"Scoop poop?" he said with all seriousness, which did nothing to lift the burning sensation from my face. He didn't dwell on my failed joke. Instead, he quickly changed the subject, "So," he leaned forward with his palms pressed firmly on the table in front of him. "I've been thinking about something ever since I walked you home the other night, and I wanted to ask you . . ."

"Yeah," my voice came out super-high pitched. It was bittersweet because I had finally broken past the distracted filter he was carrying around and we were connecting. But not like a normal friend thing. This was my breath was locked in my chest, over what I might accidentally say sort of connection. Even though, I'd literally had *thousands* of conversations with Fulton in my life, I couldn't deny that something was different for us. It wasn't about Candace's constant text messages, but it had everything to do with how he got flustered when he tried to explain Candace to me. And it wasn't about us being back in the same city again, but it was everything to do with us trying to carve out private time for each other despite our separate lives. But mostly, it was about the way he kept sneaking these intense gazes on me, and how I melted into a giant pool of putty every time he did it.

If I had to be honest, I had been curious about Fulton since we said goodbye in Montana. The more I studied the expression he was giving me, the more my curiosity grew. I felt so totally clueless. The heat cranked up even more on my cheeks. *I wasn't even saying anything!* I put my head down and slurped out of my drink cup, trying to cool the warmth in my face. It wasn't that I hadn't ever had a crush before either. I had dated before I went to Montana, but all those relationships were easy. Looking back on it though, they were easy because I really wasn't emotionally connected to those guys the way I was with Fulton. With Fulton—I was just so exposed. He knew my whole story—even the parts I would have preferred to keep private. Here we were, steeped in this silence. He was watching me as I pretended to fiddle with my drink cup.

I carefully selected my words. Then with the utmost of caution, I dared myself to look at his face and cleared my throat. "Okay . . ." I started, and my voice was still embarrassingly high-pitched, so I cleared it one more time. By now, Fulton was giving me his full attention, and I felt my face light up like a glow bug again!

He kept looking at me, like he was waiting for me to say something intelligent, but that wasn't happening. I needed to pause so I could work through my brain fog. I grabbed my drink cup again and slurped down another few drinks while looking over the straw at him, wondering what in the universe I was going to say next. I could see an animation in his eyes telling me he had *exactly* the same feelings that I was also now remembering from the night he had walked me home. Totally speechless, I just sat here overjuiced from this stupid cherry-drink, and an inability to use my words. I set my cup back, but the bottom of the cup brushed across the edge of the table, tipping it over, spilling the drink out like wildfire all over Fulton's lap!

His mouth dropped down in a sudden shock as he stood to get out of my cherry drink waterfall. *It was too late.* Frantically leaning forward, I collected my cup, but it was already empty. My palm slapped my mouth, and I cried out, "I'm so sorry," when I saw his red-stained pants. I grabbed my stack of napkins and pushed them toward him.

"It's okay," he muttered, as he took my napkins and tried to clean up as discretely as he could. After only a second, in a voice that was barely even audible to me, he said, "I need to change."

"Yeah," I clumsily got out of our booth. "I'm sorry," I squeaked out again. It wasn't that getting a drink spilled on you was overly embarrassing. We were both stunned from the timing of *when* it happened. We were about to break through a wall that boxed us in as only friends. If there was a void anywhere in this universe, I desperately wanted it to be beneath my feet so it could swallow me up. But there wasn't a void, and I hurriedly collected my garbage, and dumped it into the trash, muttered a super-fast goodbye to Fulton as we parted ways. I practically ran home, boosted from the remnants of my super-juice buzz not sure if I should cry from humiliation, or shout out in joy because I couldn't deny it anymore. Maybe it didn't happen tonight, but something was definitely happening to Fulton and I. We were definitely going to be more than friends. *If only I could have been just a tad bit more smooth . . .*

Chapter Nine

The next morning, my stomach was a wreck over the anticipation of fashion week. Gabby's insomnia must have rubbed off on me. After lying awake most of the night, I finally decided to get up. Since I was running early, I grabbed expensive, frothy coffees and tried to psych myself up for whatever was going to be thrown my way. The sun was still waking when I arrived, but Gabby looked like she had hours of work behind her already. She sat at her desk with reading glasses on, flipping through papers filled with tiny print.

"How's it going?" I treaded lightly when I set her coffee on her desk, hoping it would be a good enough bribe for her to not be mad at me anymore.

"You read my mind." She immediately picked up her cup and took a sip. I padded softly to my desk and set my purse—now purposely crammed full of snacks since I realized eating at regular intervals was not a real thing in this office—down next to my coffee. "I think I'm catching a break," she said and stretched her arms high over her head like she hadn't moved in hours.

"What happened?"

"I was up all night, researching manufacturers and doing budgets, and I think I found a way I can keep my wage matrix as is, plus bring a couple more seamstresses onboard to meet my freight demands *and* have extra money for a larger rent payment."

"You were up all night?"

"I was." She nodded a little woefully but then quickly pivoted her attention back to her desk and picked up a sheet of paper, reaching it over to me. "But it was worth it because my head's in a better place now. I looked at a couple retail spaces last night with the realtor, and this is a contract agreement for one."

I reached forward, receiving the sheet, a little scared of what it might say because I now knew everything "crazy" she did had a direct effect on what I would have to do. "Retail?"

"That's part of my plan. I keep losing store contracts because they're going out of business. I've been having to absorb unsold inventory and take a loss because by the time I get it back, it's out of season. I can't do that anymore. Department stores used to be a bridge to my customers. Now they're like this giant roadblock to my financial freedom."

"You have to do something to get your clothes out there, though," I said.

"This isn't working. It's a slow bleed." She refreshed her sales screen on her computer and pointed to the total. "The sales are up now, but how long before people forget again? Then it dawned on me after you left yesterday. Yes, we need a bigger space. I want more control of my inventory flow, but my main issue is lack of visibility. All this PR made my sales spike because I've been visible. I need that all the time. I never thought it was going to work to have my own store because of all the overhead, but with my high-end line launching, I have more than enough product to fill a whole store. So, it's time."

I grinned approvingly at her. "Go big or go home."

She flashed me a look like she was the last batter headed up to bat in the final inning in the world series and the game was tied. "Yep, I'd have to say if this doesn't work, nothing will."

"So, you found a spot?" I asked.

"I did. Right on Fifth Avenue."

I arched an eyebrow. "Seriously?"

"Yep, I'm maxing out my line of credit for the down payment, but like you said, it's go big or go home."

"I hope this works, because I really don't want to go home," I said to her but more to myself. The thought of having to live with my mom made tension pool in the front of my brain. I'd do everything within my power to make sure Gabby's plan was a success. I decided to dig right in, so I asked, "What do you need me to do today?"

"Great question." She another grabbed a clipboard and handed it to me. "Let's have a quick meeting to organize." I scanned the list with so many items on that it looked like a one-month plan, not a week. "Our showcase isn't until Wednesday, and I have everything done for that," she started.

"Good," I said.

"I got the sketches for our giveaway dress done this morning, and I sent them off for a sample. Once they are back, I'll have you run to pick them up, and if you could get in contact with our winner for a fitting, that'll be great."

"I can do that." I grabbed my favorite purple pen and wrote a note to myself in my work planner.

"I told her to put a rush on that sample, so if you don't hear anything by Monday, call her." I jotted another note and enjoyed how my page was quickly filling with more purple ink. "And actually, now that I'm looking this over . . ." She ran her fingers along her planner. "I have so many interviews and shows I need to be at that I plan to be down at the park most of the time. If I could delegate that whole project of the unveiling of the dress and everything to you, that would really be helpful."

"Absolutely, I'll let you know if I need anything, but I can take care of it."

"The other thing that is high priority is I need you to check in with Mia, our pregnant model, the night before our showcase. I want one last fitting so there are no surprises." Her eyes held mine. "Can you handle that too? Then I can cross that off my list."

"Got it." I wrote another note to myself.

"Okay, so here's where we're going to feel pinched." She paused, waiting for me to stop writing. "I have over two hundred cases of freight for our new line arriving today through Tuesday. I've passed a copy of this contract over to my lawyer, and I told my real estate agent I need access to retail space now. She's going to talk to the owner to see if I can get a key today so I can have those crates dropped off there."

I scanned our studio that already had shelves and stacks lining all four walls. "That would be great if we could do that. Then we don't have to worry about moving them later."

"Exactly." She pointed her pen at me. "The website for that line goes live Wednesday after our showcase, so that's when we need to be ready to start shipping. I need those cases unpacked and organized." She bit her lip and stared at me like whatever she was thinking was painful, and then she added, "I need to delegate that to you too."

I tried not to flinch. "You want me to unpack two hundred cases of freight by Wednesday?"

"I do. I don't have another option because I need Sanita to keep up with the regular line of freight here."

"What happens if I can't get a key?"

"You break a window," she said with a straight face.

"Okay . . ." I hid my eyes by pretending to write more notes, but I didn't need to write this down. It's like having to point out the beached whale in the middle of the road. "So," I started in a casual voice, "you don't mind if I put in a few hours this weekend then?"

She chuckled. "You'll be lucky to have a few hours off."

"Got it. Anything else you need me to handle?" I held my breath.

"If you can do all that, I'll be amazed."

"Don't worry." I set my clipboard back on my desk. "I got it covered." Then without wasting time, I picked up my phone and started searching for numbers. "First, I'll try to get a hold of the delivery service to see if we can change our drop-off site." I found the number I needed and hesitated to press send as I had a sudden urge to call 911 to scream for help. Thankfully, I was able to resist that urge and got to work instead.

Chapter Ten

After workathoning my butt off all weekend, I woke up on Tuesday morning panicked because I still had so much to do. I was at the store before the sun had a chance to wink at me.

I pushed the stacks of empty totes against one wall and counted the full totes as I reorganized the stacks. Thirty-seven totes left and I had to leave at noon for the two fittings. I couldn't unpack that many totes if I worked straight for the next twenty-four hours. I pulled out my phone and sent a group text to Becky and Tina.

Me: *Hey girls, I know you have school today but is there any way you'd want to stop over at Gabby's new store after school and help me unpack freight? I could really use the help.*

Becky: *Sure, I can stop.*

Tina: *It's so weird you have to do all that work.*

Me: *Thanks, Becky. Can't wait to see you. Tina, you in?*

Tina: *I suppose I can come with Becky.*

Me: *Thank you!*

I tucked my phone away and grabbed another tote to unpack. Part of me was relieved to have backup coming, but the other part of me knew to not be fooled because Tina and Becky had never worked a day in their life. Their ability to be productive didn't seem reliable. However, I had to believe it would be okay because I didn't see any other options.

I blazed through my totes, making sure each garment was hung perfectly and neatly stowed on a rack. I hated that I had to quit at noon, but I had an appointment to meet the model, Mia. I carried a garment bag with her dress in one hand, and with the other, I pulled random snacks from my purse and wolfed them down as I raced to Bryant Park. I found Mia crouched over a trashcan, puking.

"You're still sick?" I asked when she came up for air.

She wiped her chin with a tissue she had been clenching. "It's a nightmare. I was fine until I got on stage, and then I got dizzy. It was scorching and crowded in the tent, and I was low on oxygen."

"Did you call your doctor?"

"Yeah, my husband insisted I check in with her. She continues to say it's normal and actually considered healthy." Her eyes drifted to the garment bag I had draped over my arm. "You got my dress?"

"Yeah, this should not take too long." I used my free hand to help her off the ground.

"I'll sneak behind that curtain." She took the bag, and after a minute called out to me, "It feels the same to me."

I pulled the curtain back and ran my fingers along the seam in the back of the dress, feeling for gaps or pinching, but it was perfect. "I think you're good. She did a nice job with your alterations."

"She always does." Mia agreed and slipped the dress off over her head and handed it to me.

I hung it back in the bag. "I'll hold onto this and meet you here tomorrow."

"Sounds good. See you tomorrow."

I waved goodbye and left the tent. Checking my phone, I found text messages from Tina and Becky, who were both on their way to the store. They walked up just as I arrived.

"Abs! I can't believe you're a career woman," Becky said.

I unlocked the door and let them inside. "I don't know about career. It feels more like work." I had meant it as a joke, but then I realized it was actually the truth.

"So, what's the gossip on the store?" Becky asked as they both followed me inside.

"She wants to have it ready to open by Christmas, but we need to get everything moved from our office in the next couple weeks, so it will be a tight schedule."

Tina strolled over to a round clothing rack and flipped through the row of shirts. "What's it like to work for a designer?" she asked.

I locked the door behind me, turned on the rest of the lights, and hung Mia's dress on the rack closest to the door. "I haven't had time to think about it."

"Is that the fashion week dress?" Tina asked, moving toward it in a curious manner.

"It is."

"Can we see it?"

I unzipped the bottom so they could peek at the fabric. "Everything in this show has gold lace on it," I explained as I held it out for them to see.

"You wouldn't let me try it on, would you?" Tina asked.

I folded the bottom of my lip in for a moment. "Nah, I better not. It's tailored for Mia. It wouldn't fit you anyway."

"What do you need us to do?" Becky asked as she took a few steps around the edge of the store, looking at all the racks.

"Good question." I zipped the garment bag closed and walked to my stack of totes. Then I flung one open and dragged it to rest at Becky's feet. "All these totes need to be emptied. It's pretty simple. Just tear off all the plastic, hang up everything, and try to group them with the rest of the pieces that match."

Becky got right to work ripping off plastic. I tied a trash bag on her rack for her and then pushed a tote over to another rack for Tina, who seemed more interested in shopping than working. "Did you see this dress?" she pulled out a sand-colored day dress with a maroon belt.

"I love that one," I agreed, but I didn't waste time talking. I dragged another tote out and opened it.

"Can I try it on?" Tina asked.

I cringed at her request. Any other time, I would have been fine with them playing dress up, but I was pressed for time. Nothing can go wrong this week. Gabby trusted me, and I needed to prove to her that I was worthy of that trust. "I rather you wouldn't. This is her high-end line, and everything's expensive," I explained.

"Come on, Abs. Just this one?" Tina pressed.

Becky's face slacked as she looked at me and then Tina. "She said no. Just hang it back up before Abs gets in trouble."

Tina's face flushed as she rehung the dress, reached into the tote and started to sullenly work through the freight.

After working for a while in silence, it hit me that I hadn't taken a break in hours. "I have to go to the bathroom," I said. Then I practically ran back to the bathroom. When I flipped the light on, I deflated when I saw myself in the mirror. My skin was dried, and makeup had settled into the cracks on my forehead and new dark shadows lined the bottom of my eyelids. I splashed cold water on my face, careful to not wet my bandage but hoping to spring some life into my paling skin. I wiped the excess water away but only succeeded in smearing what was left of my cracked makeup. Before I had time to wipe it off, the buzzer rang on the door. I hurried, crossing my fingers, hoping it wasn't more freight. Then forced a smiled when I saw it was the giveaway winner. "Hi, Romana," I said when I let the middle-aged woman inside the store.

Her smile was contagious, like a tiny lift setting me on a path to a better mood. "I can't wait to see my dress," she squealed, her eyes shining brightly.

I motioned toward Tina and Becky. "These are my friends. They are helping me." I nodded back to Romana. "This is Romana. She needs to do a quick fitting before our big reveal tomorrow."

Tina and Becky waved at her but didn't say anything.

I grabbed Romana's garment bag from the rack and motioned for her to follow. "Come on back here," I said. Then I hung the bag in the bathroom, leaving the light on for her as I exited. "Slip it on and open the door when you are ready for me to check." Then in my first real break in hours, I slumped into the corner to wait and pulled out my phone finding a message from Fulton, and as I read it, my mouth fell open. I'd forgotten it was his birthday! He was inviting me to a dinner with his friends. I rubbed my forehead and silently scolded myself. I was upset that I would have to miss the dinner and even more upset that I'd forgotten his birthday altogether.

As I finished a lengthy text back to Fulton explaining why I had to decline his invitation, Romana walked out of the bathroom. Her dress was yellow and flowy in all the right places, but my eyes focused on an unsightly gathering of fabric below her arm holes. I tugged the seam to pull it tighter and explained, "This needs to come in here." I reached for the sewing kit I had stashed on the bathroom shelf and dug out the tray of stick pins. "Can you hold your arm up? I'll pin it to where it needs to be adjusted."

She eagerly obliged. "Good thing you had that sewing kit handy."

"Right? I learned fast that I can't ever be too prepared for these fittings." I stuck a couple pins in a row and then stepped back to examine the dress from the side.

"Is it going to be ready for tomorrow?" she asked.

"It should. I'll have to drop it off at the tailors, but this is an easy fix."

She smoothed the dress out with her hands. "I love how it feels."

"It's all yours after tomorrow." I circled around to her back. "Stand still and I'll help you out of it so you don't get stuck by a pin." I unzipped her and carefully pulled the dress over her head and hung it back in the bag. "Come out front when you're ready," I called as I shut the door behind me and went to check on the girls.

Becky had finished her tote and was hanging out by the front door. Her eyes shifted around the room before landing on me. "What's up?" I asked.

"I need to go. I have studying to do, but thanks for letting us see your new store."

Tina appeared from behind a clothing rack, and she had her purse flung over her shoulder, ready to leave too. "You have to leave too?" I grimaced because, between the two of them, they only got two totes done.

"Yeah, Benson wants me to meet him for some ice cream, and we haven't seen each other since Friday night."

"Okay," I said in a defeated voice. I walked to the door to let them out and forced myself to smile. "Thanks for helping."

"No prob, anytime," Tina said as she walked out first.

"Call us when you want to go out," Becky said over her shoulder.

"I will." I smiled at them through the glass door, knowing I would never call them to go out. My life was all about work now. I turned to face my stacks of totes, and my throat got tight. *I'll never get this done by tomorrow.* I accepted defeat and sat on the floor to Gabby.

"Abs, how's it going?" she greeted me after only one ring.

"Alright. I got Mia's dress fitted, and it's perfect."

"Good."

"And I got Romana's dress fitted. It needs a slight alteration, but the tailor is working late because of fashion week so I'll drop it off."

"Perfect, and how's freight?"

"I can't do it," I rushed out before I lost my nerve. "I worked all weekend, and I'm still here now, but it's not going to be done by tomorrow and I feel terrible." I sucked my bottom lip in, waiting for her to get mad.

"How much did you get done?"

"About two-thirds," I quickly estimated.

"Well . . ." She paused, and I heard a sigh. "That's the way it goes sometimes. I can send Sanita over first thing in the morning, because I'm going to need you here for the showcase. We'll have to make it work."

"I'll come back after I drop this dress off at the tailors and work as late as I can," I offered.

"That'll be good. Every little bit helps. Thank you."

"You're welcome," I said but I still felt like I was a huge disappointment, so I added, "Sorry."

"These things happen."

"Thanks for understanding. I'll see you tomorrow at the tent." I ended the call, dropped my phone into my bag and stared at the wall. "This stinks," I said to myself. However, I didn't have time to dwell on my failure. It was time to speed walk to the tailors to drop off Romana's dress. It was surprisingly helpful for me to get out of the store in the fresh air. I was in a good mood by the time I returned, ready to start my night shift, working freight. To my surprise, when I got back to the store, Fulton, Wally, and Candace were waiting outside. "How come you guys are here?" I asked when I came up on their approach.

Fulton beamed at me. "We were done with dinner. Everyone else left to see a movie, but I wanted to see you. So, these guys offered to come with me, and we decided to surprise you and help out." He leaned closer to me, and his eyes searched my face when he asked, "If that's okay?"

"It's your birthday. You don't have to waste your night helping me."

"You helped me at the vet clinic, so I owe you one," Fulton said.

My cheeks started to preheat again when I remembered how the other night had ended. I let out of hard breath, trying to stay cool.

"Psssh." I waved my hand in a dismissing manner. "That was a synch."

"We want to," Wally interjected. "I feel like I owe you one too since I caused so much drama."

It was easy to smile now that the eviction had worked out for the better and Gabby had benefited from the attention. "You don't owe me any favors," I replied. "And you were sorta funny." I scanned the three of them, a gentle relief started to bud in my chest, knowing they were here to help. I didn't want to give them any reasons to change their minds, I quickly said, "Since you're all here, you don't have to ask twice." I held the door open for them. "I'll take any help I can get."

Fulton was the last to go through the door, and when he did, I asked, "Are you having a good birthday?"

"Yeah, I wanted to spend it with my friends . . . and to see you." He gave me the sweetest, shy smile I had ever seen; it instantly filled my heart with a giddy, teenage-girl-scream that I did everything I could do to not let out. Thankfully, he kept talking, "So, I'd say I'm having a good one." His eyes moved to scan the room, then he asked, "How can we help?"

"Er . . . Grab a tote and hang up the clothes inside of it," I explained. And just like that, the trio got to work, and everything flowed well with our new teamwork.

It was after ten when I heard keys in the door. Gabby appeared and her eyes narrowed when she saw us. "What's going on?" she asked.

"Hi." I stood up straight. "These are my friends." I motioned to the group. "They're helping me get the freight done." I pointed to the last single stack of totes left. "It's almost done."

"Wow, nice friends." Gabby's brow softened. She walked to a rack and fanned through the clothes. "Everything looks nice. You guys are doing a good job." Then she crossed the floor to another rack and stopped next to Wally, raising a disapproving eyebrow at him. "I recognize this guy. You're the roach."

He smiled sheepishly. "I'm sorry about the eviction. I had no idea something like that could happen."

"It's fine." She looked back to the rack in front of her. "You actually made me a lot of money."

"His name is Wally," I said. "And that's Fulton and Candace." I motioned to them individually.

Gabby kept her chin down as she flipped through hangers, meticulously scanning each garment, but she did manage to say, "Thanks for your help, guys. This all looks great." Then after a short pause, she suggested, "Abs, if you want to submit a time slip for your friends, we can pay them out as casual labor."

I nodded agreeingly.

"I love your clothes," Candace commented, smiling at Gabby in a way-too-obvious-buttering up manner, but I didn't care because I was all for it if it helped put Gabby in a good mood. "This dress over here is stunning."

"Which one?" Gabby moved closer to Candace, who held up an A-lined dress with sheer blush-colored layers that started at the floor and gathered into a side wrap at the waist.

"I love how that one turned out too." Gabby admired it, checking the seams and the length of each layer.

"That has to be one of my favorites too," I agreed. "The skirt reminds me of how a rose blooms."

Gabby turned to me. "Do you like it?"

"Yeah, it's gorgeous."

She held it up to my shoulders. "It would look stunning on you with your dark hair."

"If I ever had somewhere to wear it too."

She held it out toward me. "You can have it."

I blinked. "What?"

"You need something to wear tomorrow when you're down at the park with me. A lot of people are going to see you when you do the live reveal too. We don't want to waste an opportunity to show off my new line. Unless you want a different one?"

"No, that's the prettiest one here." I lightly touched the fabric. "Are you sure?" I raised my now nervous eyes to meet hers, not sure of why she was giving me this gift, but completely willing to receive it.

"Take it." She waved me away and turned her attention back to Candace, asking her opinion about other items.

I carried the dress to the front of the store and hung it next to the rest of my stuff. My inner sixteen-year-old self was doing cartwheels and trying not to scream! This was the prettiest dress I had ever laid eyes on. Not only was it mine to wear but I was gifted it by the designer who made it! I'm dead.

I forced myself to walk away (still doing leaps and twirls in my head) and went back to one of the last totes. Everyone worked with a sense of urgency, and I could tell we were impressing Gabby by the way she kept scanning the group and then nodding to herself. After another hour, Gabby spoke up. "It's late, everybody. We can be done. I can have Sanita finish these last totes in the morning." She grabbed her purse. "Plus, I need to make another trip back to the studio before I can get home, so I need to take off." She waved.

"Thanks for the amazing work, guys. Just leave stuff as it is and go home."

"See you tomorrow." I waved. Then I turned to Candace, who was standing the closest to me. "Thank you so much for helping me," I told her as sincerely as I could. "If you ever need a favor, don't hesitate to ask."

She closed her tote, pushing it back against the wall. "No problem. It was sort of fun." Then she tucked her hands into her coat pockets, waiting by the door for the guys who were finishing their totes. I did a floor check, shutting off the lights. Then I remembered to tuck my sewing kit into my purse for tomorrow, grabbed Mia's and my dresses, and we all walked out together.

"We're all headed in the opposite direction of you," Fulton said. "Are you okay walking home by yourself?"

I twisted the key in the lock, then yanked on the door to check that it was secured and said, "I'll be fine."

"Okay." Fulton lingered in the back of the group, looking like he wanted to talk but then he caught of glimpse of the group getting way ahead and it seemed like he settled on saying, "Good luck tomorrow with your big show. It'll be great."

"I hope so." I lowered my eyes and smiled as sweetly as my exhausted self could. "And again, *thank you*. I'm sure this wasn't what you had in mind for your birthday celebration, but I couldn't have done all this without you guys." I looked at Wally and Candace now halfway down the block, and called out, "You guys are amazing! Thanks!"

They waved, and I lifted my eyes back to Fulton, who had a serious expression on his face. "I owed you one anyway."

I had intended to give Fulton an appreciative smile, and then say goodnight but when I looked up at him, his eyes were fixated on me in that way he had recently started doing. I was now thoroughly convinced this was a new superpower he had gained, and he was using it against me with the sole purpose to completely disable me. *My feet froze to the ground, and my words instantly died in my chest.* Then he added to his comment, "and I wanted to see you."

I opened my mouth to respond, but my words were still stuck under his demobilizing superpower and all that came out was a shallow fog of a breath. My eyes skirted to see Candace and Wally right up the street, waiting for Fulton. I wasn't a hundred percent sure what was happening with Fulton and I, but I had a pretty good guess. I definitely didn't feel comfortable feeling these feelings with two nosey peepers gawking. In a faint voice, I tried to speak in private, "I'm glad I got to see you too." I tilted my head toward our audience. "But I think they are waiting."

Fulton edged away from the door. "Well . . . yeah, I see that."

I cleared my throat, "Um, give me a couple days to get caught up. We will have to do something fun to celebrate your birthday," I offered.

"Deal." He let his eyes linger on mine for one long curious moment, and then he scurried after Candace and Wally. I rechecked the lock on the door, then let my back rest against it for a moment, drinking in deep breaths. I couldn't believe my mind. I had almost completed the impossible. Although I was exhausted, I had the feeling of success. Sure, I needed some help, but I was able to do my job. As exhausted as I felt, I was happy—no, I was exuberant about what I had accomplished. Nothing about this week had been easy, but that made the success even sweeter. I rested the back of my head against the door while I took a few moments to bask in the sweet glories of victory. Then I headed home, *wondering what was up with Fulton . . .*

Chapter Eleven

The next morning was gloomy, gross gray with misting clouds, but I arrived at the tent early with more than enough time to do Romana's dress reveal. While I waited for Mia, I assisted Gabby's other models, making sure their dresses were flawless. I rechecked my watch anxiously and was relieved when I saw Mia hurrying through the mobs of people toward me.

"Sorry," she said with a strained look on her face. "Mornings are still super hard for me, and hair and makeup were backed up."

I held her garment bag out for her. "Are you feeling any better?"

"Not really." She took the bag. "You look gorgeous, though."

"Thanks." I smoothed the skirt of my dress. I knew my sixteen-year-old self was still off doing infinity twirls somewhere to celebrate this dress. I didn't hide my excitement. With a huge smile I said, "Gabby gave me the dress for free PR."

She pointed to my forehead. "And you took your bandage off."

"Yes, I did that this morning. The stitches were gone. I put a little powder over the red part, so hopefully it sticks out less than before."

"It looks great," she echoed again then moved behind the curtain. I listened to her shuffle, then she added, "I ran into Gabby when I was getting my makeup. She should be on her way over. What the . . ." Her voice trailed off.

"Do you need my help?" I leaned toward the curtain, scared she was going to throw up.

"It looks like someone took a giant hacksaw to the skirt on my dress!"

"What do you mean?" I pushed the curtain aside and stepped behind it. I reached out and held the fabric up to see where long slits appeared. "What the . . ." I dropped one fabric piece and frantically picked up another one. "Here's another slit and another . . ." Astonished, my heart now pounding as I combed through the fabric with my fingers. "I can't believe this," I said, seeing the entire skirt had been shredded like a hula skirt.

"You ladies back here?" Gabby's voice rang out.

"I'm helping Mia with her dress but there's a problem . . ." I called from behind the curtain.

"It doesn't fit?" her voice came closer.

I stepped out from behind the curtain with the dress in my arms. "She doesn't have it on." I held up one of the pieces of skirt to show how it was sliced.

Gabby covered her mouth with her hand. "What happened?" She took the dress from me and looked closely at the slits. "Who cut this?"

"You think it's been cut?" I asked.

"Well, yeah. You can see the straight edge of a scissor in the cuts." She pointed to the openings. "If it were torn, the fabric would at least be a little frayed. You can't rip something that straight either."

She flipped the dress over, examining it. "I tell you, I've been doing this for twenty years, and I've been through just about everything, but this is the first time I've had to go through someone sabotaging me." She glared at me. "Who had access to this dress?"

I shrugged my tense shoulders. "Nobody. I've had it the whole time. It was fine yesterday when we did our fitting, and I took it back to the store yesterday."

"You had friends at the store when I was there." She leaned closer to me in what I felt was an accusatory manner. "What about that girl? She seemed pretty interested in my dresses."

"Candace? I don't know. She was quiet while she worked. I don't think she'd have a reason to—" I covered my mouth. "Please don't fire me." I tensed like I was trying to get smaller and disappear. I had done everything I was supposed to do this week. I had guarded that dress like a hawk. This wasn't supposed to happen like that, but this was my fault!

"What?" Gabby asked.

"I had my other friends there first."

"You think they'd do something like this?"

"I don't know, but they did leave in a hurry after I was in the back room with Romana for a while."

"Well, this wasn't an accident. It's a little amateur and reeks of a high-school prank. I have every right to call the police to report this. It's vandalism." She checked the clock on her phone. "I don't have time to run back to the studio to grab a different dress either. I'm going to have to run the show with five models. Go ahead and get your clothes back on," Gabby called to Mia. "This dress is trash."

"Can you use my dress?" I asked her in a small voice that was weakening as the conversation went on.

Gabby took an exacerbated sigh and curled her lip in before glancing back at me. "Nah, it's the wrong fit and would be too short on Mia." Then she turned her shoulder away from me. *She was blaming me.* My heart slammed against my ribcage.

I let her down.

There's no way I can get fired.

I'd have to go back to the farm, and I'd rather die!

"I can fix it," I blurted out.

"How are you going to fix this? It's shredded worse than a paper shredder." She pulled on the slits again.

"I can sew panels into it." My mind raced as I planned the design in my head. "Please, let me try," I begged.

The skin between her eyebrows pulled together in contemplation. "What are you thinking?"

"I'll sew a piece of triangular fabric into the slits to form a skirt. I won't have time to patch all the slits, so some of them will just have to be like fringe for decoration. It'll give it more of a full train, but it would look really cool." I tried to sound excited about it, hoping she'd buy into it. I frantically dug in my purse for my sewing kit, grabbed my scissors and aimed at the first sheer layer of my own dress.

Gabby gasped. "Are you cutting your dress?"

"I need some fabric for the patches, and this layer will be perfect."

"You'd better not. You need to look presentable." She held her hand out to block my scissors. "It'll be fine. I'll run the show with the five models we have. I know you feel bad, but I need these dresses to be perfect and not look like someone's craft project."

I pushed her hand aside and cut into my dress, retrieving the first patch. Then I held the patch under one of Mia's slits. "This'll look cool. Trust me. I know what I'm doing. If it doesn't work out, then Mia won't walk, but you weren't going to use her anyway, so it won't be anything lost."

The look of shock on Gabby's face told me that she didn't really trust me, but I could tell she wasn't going to stop me. After watching me cut out another patch from my skirt, she said, "Well, what do we have to lose then? Let me help you." She dropped to the floor next to me, grabbed my sewing needle and went to work while I cut another patch. My mind plotted almost as fast as my hands worked. I prayed this was a good idea and quietly thanked Linda in my head for forcing me to sew all those patches on everything last year. I would have never thought sewing patches would be a skill I would need, but as of right now, it was all that was keeping me from being fired. I prayed it was enough.

Chapter Twelve

"Gabby said both your crisis skills and sewing skills were amazing," my dad said.

It was Saturday morning, my first real day off, and I was still lying in my bed. I adjusted my phone for comfort and replied, "I felt terrible."

"I can't believe Tina and Becky turned on you like that either. Do you have any idea why?"

"I don't really know," I said. "I haven't talked to them except for that one day. They didn't seem mad." I let my mind wander through other pranks the girls had played on people over the years even though they weren't funny pranks. Tina and Becky were never funny girls. They did it because they were mean girls. That's all they ever were. I could see now that's all they'd ever be.

"I guess you know who your real friends are," my dad said after silence.

"I guess so." I didn't want to talk about them anymore, so I changed the subject. "How's Mom?"

"She's enjoying being back home. She has a different therapist, who has all these new strategies, and they are meeting a couple times a week. I'm hopeful it'll work this time." I didn't believe he was hopeful. Hopeful was the word we used to talk about my mom's condition, but it could be easily substituted for the word *tolerated*. We tolerated her condition. My phone beeped from a text coming in, but I ignored it.

"How's school?" His question was a lightning bolt flashing on a dark night, suddenly making all that was hidden visible. I hadn't completely forgotten about school, but I had been giving myself permission to put it off since I was working so much. "Your silence is telling me it's not going well," Dad said.

"Or . . ."

"Or what?"

"Or, I haven't had time for it yet."

"What do you mean?" His voice ticked up a notch, but I could tell it was more from stress than anger. "That's the one condition I gave you when I allowed you this privilege. You haven't done anything? You've got to be two weeks behind again."

"I'm sorry." I sat up in my bed. "I was completely caught off guard with this job. I thought it would be easy and I could do my assignments while I held down the office. I honestly have barely sat down since I got here. But I can look at it today. I promise I'll look at it as soon as I get off the phone."

"I appreciate your honesty even though you haven't gotten off to the best start. I'll let you go so you have time to get caught up today."

"I will," I woefully agreed.

We ended our chat, and I checked my text message. It was Fulton.

Fulton: *You want to go to the theatre tonight to watch Wally?*

Me: *It's not Wednesday.*

Fulton: *They have a special variety show tonight with some of their regulars.*

I let my thumbs hover over my phone. I had promised my dad I would get caught up with school. *I missed having fun.* I needed to do something to destress. The past week had been a nightmare. Before I could talk myself out of it, I replied.

Me: *Sure. I'll meet you there.*

I hit send before I could change my mind. Then I got up, gathered my laundry and my laptop, and hurried to the laundromat to kill two birds with one stone.

I wasn't surprised to see Candace sitting in the seat next to Fulton when I arrived at the theatre, but I was overwhelmingly bummed. I snagged one of the empty chairs across from them. "Hey, thanks for saving me a seat," I said to Fulton when I scooted my chair closer to the table.

"You're welcome," Fulton said.

I looked around and the place was empty compared to the last time I was there. "Who else is coming?"

"Just us," Fulton said, "and Wally. He'll join us after his segment."

I nodded. "Cool." I was about to attempt to make small talk with Candace, but she had started a quiet conversation with Fulton that I couldn't hear. I checked the time, and I was early. We had at least twenty minutes before the show, and my stomach was growling. I excused myself to get something from concessions.

Now standing in line, I tried to figure out what the best value pack deal would be. I was debating on a number two, which included a small popcorn, a small drink, and a candy, or a number three, which included a small drink, small popcorn, and mini donuts. I stretched to try to see what the donuts looked like. If they had powdered sugar, I'd have to go with those. If they didn't have powdered sugar, I would get the other option with Dots. The line moved, and there was only one more couple in front of me.

"Aubergine," Wally's voice called from in front of the line. Narrowing my eyes for focus, I saw that he was working behind the counter, filling soda cups.

I waved and waited until it was my turn to order before asking, "So you work concessions here too?"

He gave me his mischievous grin. "Yeah, usually they run one guy here, but the place's packed tonight, so I volunteered to help with the preshow rush. Hey, come here a sec." He waved me over to the side counter. I followed him thinking he was going to hook me up with free snacks. He unhooked the little door and pushed it open. "Come on back. You can help too."

"Oh no." Taking a giant step back, I insisted, "This is my night off."

"You don't really have to do anything. Just stand here and hang out. You can talk to the customers while they wait so they don't get mad."

"Aren't there rules against random people hanging out behind the counter while you work?"

"Nah, nobody will notice." He opened a pantry door, pulled out a red apron and tried handing it to me. "Here, throw this on, and you'll blend right in."

I looked back at the customers stacking up with only one person helping them now. "You'd better get back to work." I took a step back toward the line.

His eyes pleaded. "I helped you at your job."

"Oh, so this is payback?"

"Not really. Come on." He waved me inside the door again. I have no idea why—maybe it was because I didn't want to have to be the third wheel at the table with Fulton and Candace or maybe I felt like I owed him a favor—but I walked forward and took the apron.

"You can fill drinks because that's the easiest." He flashed a half-grin as he ushered me to my new station. He walked to the till and rang up the next customer who ordered a large drink. I retrieved the large plastic cup, scooped ice into it, and then set it on the tray and pressed the fill button. The soda ran and then stopped. I waited for the fizz to go down and like I had seen many times before, the machine automatically applied another spritz of soda to top it off. I put the lid on and gave it to the customer.

"Nice job," Wally said.

I smiled at myself for being able to complete such a simple task of service. The old Abs would have never been caught dead working a concession stand and wearing a service apron, It was sort of fun to be behind the counter, listening to people chat about the upcoming show. After a few people passed through the line, I felt comfortable asking customers for their orders. So, when Wally got backed up with a large order, I stepped in to help an adorable couple with matching gray hair. The man was wearing suspenders and a tweed newsboy hat. The woman wore a silk scarf tied at the collar of a ruffled blouse that was tucked into a twill pencil skirt that surprisingly coordinated back to the man's hat. I moved to the front counter and asked, "What can I get you two?"

The man watched me with a twinkle in his eye like we were sharing a secret, and I could feel Wally's eyes on the back of my head. Something told me I was being set up, but I held my ground. When he didn't order, I pointed to the value menu. "Here's a list of the value packs, if you need help deciding."

A sly smile crept on the man's face and he looked past me back to Wally. "Where'd you find this looker at?"

"Who said I'm the one who found her?" Wally said as he filled popcorn for another order.

"She's too cute to be one of my employees."

"I don't need to explain my personal life to you," Wally said.

My cheeks warmed as I realized this was Wally's boss! I tucked my chin down and looked over at Wally, waiting for him to explain why I was there. He remained calm and finished out the order he was working on, then helped the person next in line while ignoring the predicament I was in.

The woman must have seen the embarrassment all over my face. She hooked her arm into her husband's and pulled him in the direction of the auditorium. "Don't mind him," she said to me. "He's a joker like Wally. They're two peas in a pod."

My feet were frozen to the floor. I was afraid I got Wally in trouble, but I was also annoyed Wally didn't say more to his boss to explain why I was there. They were halfway to the door when the woman looked back and asked Wally, "Are you coming to Nana's party tomorrow?"

Wally called back at her, "Yep, I'll be there." He continued to fill popcorn for the orders.

"Wait a sec." My brain worked slowly to connect the dots. "Would Nana be your grandma?"

He nodded with a dimpled smile.

"And he was your boss?" I pointed to the auditorium door.

He nodded again, then took money for the next customer in line. "Did you figure it out yet?" he asked as he brought two more sodas to the counter.

"Are you related to them?"

"They're my parents."

"Your parents." I let my mouth fall open. "Why didn't you say so?"

"I didn't think they'd blow my cover like that." He rang up another order. I listened for the drink size, then filled another soda. Wally was ringing up the last customer in line, and he handed them their red vine licorice.

I didn't wait for him to look at me. "So you work for your dad?"

"It's sort of a family business." He filled one last popcorn and soda and set them on the counter. Then he untied his apron and, looking at the other guy who was working, said, "You're on your own. We need to go." I took off my apron and handed it to him, and he threw both the aprons into a small laundry bin in the bottom of the pantry. Then he handed me the popcorn and soda. "Free food for helping."

I took the treats, still completely confused as to what had happened, but I said, "Thanks."

"Come on, let's walk and talk." He opened the little door and let us both out. "You grab a seat already?"

"I did."

"Fulton and Candace were already there, and Candace wasn't allowing you to talk to Fulton?"

I tilted my head as I looked over at him. "How'd you know?"

"I figured it out when I saw you standing in the line for concessions by yourself. I've been the third wheel for the last year. Now I'd rather work concessions. Figured you would too."

"You're right." I nodded slowly. "What's up with her?"

He gave me one of those looks like he was being asked to solve world peace. "They study together all the time because they have all the same classes, and they are both super nerds. It was fine last year because she was sort of fun, but ever since you moved to town, she's been crazy clingy. I think Fulton's too nice of a guy to say anything, but I'm about to get a cold garden hose after her. I'm so sick of it."

I giggled at the thought of her getting sprayed. "It's painful to watch her throw herself at him."

"Excruciating."

I followed him through the doors of the auditorium, down the skinny middle aisle between the row seating and to our VIP table in front of the stage. "Look who I found," I announced when I set my snacks on the table and pulled my chair back out and sat.

Fulton looked at Wally. "Don't you have to a show to do?"

"I do but I was walking Abs back to her seat." I don't think Fulton even heard Wally's reply because Candace had started to talk to him again. Wally made a face like he wanted to strangle Candace, that thankfully neither Fulton nor Candace saw, but it made me smile. Then he rolled his eyes in their direction and said, "See you guys in a bit." It was only a short pause before the lights darkened, and Wally walked out from side stage.

The fact that Fulton didn't seem to try too hard to talk to me definitely added to the humongous load of utter confusion I had toward him. On one hand, my own intuition was yelling at me that something real was happening for Fulton and I, but then there was situations like tonight where I totally felt friend zoned. Maybe I was naïve or maybe he was playing me, but even then, I could never deny that I had budding feelings for him. Those were real, and it was getting harder to ignore. I left the theatre, feeling heart sick. My heart continued to hang low all night, while I reevaluated what had happened for us. Maybe I had been misunderstanding things?

Chapter Thirteen

The following Monday, Gabby dumped colorful chocolate candies on the center of the table to share. Taking a handful for herself, she said, "So, I want to backtrack for a second now that fashion week's over, and thank you for putting up with me. You got thrown into a lot, but you handled everything beautifully. I couldn't be more impressed."

"Thank you." I digested her compliment and waited for the catch.

She sucked on a chocolate candy for a second before continuing. "I wish I could tell you we are going to slow down, but I need this store opened by December to get in on the Christmas shopping. Construction's lined up, and that shouldn't affect your job. But I do need help on staffing." She somehow managed to keep her eyes locked on mine as she ungracefully dropped another handful of candies into her mouth.

"Sure." I sat up straighter, ready to take notes in my planner. "Do you need me to advertise?"

"Yeah, place ads for a store manager. Once we hire a manager, I'll let her build her own staff."

I penciled in my assignment and replied, "That shouldn't be a problem."

"You can start pre-screening the applicants for me too. Look for someone who has a lot of experience and flexibility."

"Yeah," I agreed. "We need someone who can handle our kind of crazy."

"I knew you'd catch on well." Her eyes creased when she returned my smile. "We have two speeds: crazy and extra crazy."

I laughed heartily and snuck a few pieces of chocolate.

"Then," she continued, "I was talking to your dad about signage for the store. He's going to start putting together a few different ideas. If you want to keep tabs on that, I trust it will be amazing. I don't have the time to oversee it, so I'm happy to hand that over to you."

"I think I can handle my dad."

"Oh, and there's this." She pulled up a screen on her tablet and pushed it in front of me. "Did you see this blogger did a feature on Mia's dress?"

My eyes landed on the page, but the immediate angst that crept into my throat prevented me from reading it. "Was it good or bad?" I shifted my eyes back to her.

"She loved it. She said the peek-a-boo pleats were the highlight of the evening."

"Really?" I lightly held my chest as if to remind myself to breathe.

"Yeah, and I got an interview lined up with a magazine later this week, and they also mentioned the pleats."

"That's cool."

"It's really cool, for you."

"For me?"

"Yeah, I'm going to make sure to credit you for the design. That was all your idea. I would have tossed the dress in the trash."

I thought about that crazy day backstage, getting nostalgic for a moment thinking about how Linda had insisted I needed to learn to patch everything. Before I could get emotional, I said, "I had a friend who made me sew patches all winter last year, so I had a little practice."

"You can thank your friend, because you have made an impact. I wouldn't be surprised if you start to see copycats."

I studied the picture of Mia on the runway. The sheer pink fabric flowed out like a tiny parachute of color when Mia walked. Remembering how much I hated sewing back on the farm, I now understood that had been a tiny part of a bigger puzzle. Now that I was working with Gabby, my experience was invaluable. I enjoyed the work, something I would have never expected myself to feel.

Gabby swiped the screen on her tablet to some sketches. "Here's what I'm working on for my casual line. What do you think? I'd love some early feedback."

Gabby had used a winter palette that included warm browns, golds, beige, and soft baby blue. "I love this." I pointed to a sweater colored in a deep reddish orange. "It's very earthy. It reminds me of the scoria in my driveway in Montana."

Examining it with me, she agreed. "It does look like scoria now that you say that."

"Actually, the cowl neck gives it a whole rocky mountain feel. I want to snuggle into it with a good book and watch it snow outside."

"You have such a good brain for visualizing fashion marketing," Gabby complimented. "I can tell you hung out with your dad a lot."

"I don't know if it's anything he taught me. I just think about how I'd wear it." I swiped through the last of the sketches and handed the tablet back to her. "Nice. I can't think of anything I would do differently."

"Thanks. It'll be here before we know it." She tapped on her tablet, opening her email screen. "Do you want me to copy you on the designs so you can look at them later to see if anything comes to mind?"

"Sure." I dropped some candy into my mouth as I thought. Her designs were great, but I didn't get the same feeling I did when I looked at her couture line. Maybe I was tired or maybe I had to wait until they were made into samples that I could hold in my hands, but something was lacking; I just couldn't decide what. Then I tried to hold it back, but a lazy yawn escaped my lips. "Sorry," I concealed my opened mouth with my hand. "I'm shot today. I'll get this manager ad written and submit it to a couple places, and then do you mind if I take off early?"

"Are you feeling okay?"

"Yeah, I think I need to let these projects sink in a little before I dive into another project."

She nodded. "Sure, that happens sometimes. Stuck in transition."

Over the next few weeks, piles of applicants poured in. Every twenty-something-year-old who wanted a job in fashion must have applied. I spent my time reading resumes while trying to not break my ankles again on the construction disaster left in the store. After work I ate late dinners by myself, sitting cross-legged and barefoot on my bed, completing the minimum requirement for online school. It had also become my new tradition to fall asleep with my laptop opened and my unfinished Chinese noodles on my side table. It was a lot to juggle, but somehow, it came together.

Needless to say, I was ecstatic for a break in my routine when Fulton reappeared from his study coma and reached out a week before my birthday to make plans. Not having seen him in weeks, I couldn't think of anyone I wanted to spend the day with more. My birthday was on a Friday, and I faced off with the clock most of the day, agonizing over whether it could ever be five o'clock. I yawned for at least the hundredth time and dabbed the water that had just pooled in my eyes when Gabby walked in the door from a meeting. "How's it going?" she asked.

I sat up straighter. "It's going. I got all the orders finished. Now I'm checking a few of the references on our manager candidates."

Her eyebrows perked. "How's that?"

"Good. I honestly think we have two great gals to pick from."

"Just two?"

"I had hundreds of applicants, but when I did their phone interviews, I always found a reason to cross them off. Most of them had insane requests for banker's hours or desired expensive benefits packages and tons of time off."

"Time off?" Gabby released a sarcastic laugh. "They haven't even started yet."

"Exactly." I pointed at her in agreement. "I'd barely start the interview, and they would start telling me their lifestyle needs. I'd be like, hmm, um, that's lovely, but I'll have to check with Gabby and get back to you, and then I dumped that application in the trash."

Gabby browsed over my shoulder at the folders I had opened on my desk. "So, who do you have for me then?"

"This gal's amazing." I put my hand on the folder on the left. "She was a store manager for a purse designer for ten years, where she was promoted to district manager and did that for another eight. The designer recently closed all their shops, so she needs to start all over, but she's super sweet and optimistic." I raised my eyes to meet hers. "I love her."

"She sounds perfect."

"Yes, she is, and she's coming in for an interview Monday with you. I noticed you had a block of time in the afternoon, so I penciled her in."

"Great. Yeah, I'd love to meet her." She nodded toward my other folder. "Who's this one?"

"She's another rockstar. She was a department manager at Macy's for nine years before getting a job offer with a jeweler. She oversaw four jewelry stores until about a year ago when the owner sold them. The new owners wanted family to work in her position.

All her references are amazing. Her bosses couldn't say enough good things about her."

"Hmm, well, she sounds awesome too."

"Yep, and she was available next Monday too. I scheduled her two hours after the first one, so you'll have plenty of time to get to know each other. Hopefully it'll work out with one of them. I think they would both be amazing."

"I'm ready to have another set of hands on this store. It's getting to be too hard for me to oversee this stuff as well as produce the new line." She spoke like she was holding something in her mouth.

Swiveling my chair to shoot her a jealous look, I asked, "Are you eating candy again?"

"It's in my purse." She pointed to her desk. "I loaded up at the store. Go grab some."

"Since you insist." I reached into her purse and pulled out a bag of mixed chocolates. "Working with you has made me a sugar addict." I laughed, then added, "But I don't want to spoil my dinner. I actually have plans for once in my life to do something fun tonight." I tilted the bag and let a few round candies fall into my palm and then returned the bag to her purse.

"Oh, are you going out?"

"I am. It's my birthday, and a friend's taking me to that new Greek restaurant."

"Ah, happy birthday!" Her lips turned up. "The big eighteen. How does it feel?"

Pausing, I reflected on all the things that had happened since I moved back to New York to work. Then my memories rewound a chapter back even further to when I was in Montana and basically on my own because my dad was busy caring for my mom. "Honestly, it feels like I've already been eighteen for a long time."

"I can see that. You grew up faster than most kids."

I let her comment simmer. I felt more mature than the other kids my age. I definitely had more responsibilities than most of them. I hardly ever did anything social. I worked, studied, and did laundry. I popped the last of my candies into my mouth and sighed. I was definitely ready for some fun tonight.

"I'm going to take off early." Gabby walked over to her desk, shut down her computer, then headed toward the door with her store keys jingling in her hands. "I need to run to the cabinet store to look at some storage ideas for that back room, and I need to pick up some floor samples. If you want to finish up your reference calls and then take off early too, you can."

I beamed back at her. "Yeah, I would love that, thank you."

"For sure. Have a fantastic birthday." She waved goodbye and went outside.

Waiting until I couldn't see her through the window anymore, I then pulled out my phone. My smile was bursting off my face when I found two text messages waiting from Fulton. However, my excitement didn't last as I read the first part of his message—it was an apology for bailing on me. He had the flu. Then he said in a second text he still had reservations at the restaurant. I could use them with someone else.

Completely heart sink I wasn't going to see Fulton, what hit me just as hard was that I didn't have anyone else to go with me. I hadn't talked to Tina or Becky since the dress incident. They wouldn't care that they had hurt me. I had seen enough of their pranks to know that my reaction to their stunt would only fuel their pleasure. I had chosen to rise above it.

Other than Tina and Becky, I hadn't made any efforts to make new friends either. As I reflected on the fact that I was going to have to spend my birthday alone, it was alarming to me how much my life had changed. Formerly one of the most popular girls, now I was the girl who was alone on my birthday, headed home to do nothing. I didn't want to tell Fulton I had no other friends to call, so I texted back:

Bummer! I was looking forward to seeing you. We'll have to reschedule for another time. Feel better. Don't worry about the reservations. I won't need them tonight.

I set my phone down and organized my desk, fully aware of how eerily quiet the office was now. Blinking back self-pity tears, I shuffled my papers, organizing my desk before I got up to walk myself out of the store. This was the earliest I had gotten off work since I started. Plus, it was Friday night! I should've been rushing to have fun, not dragging my feet to the grocery store for a pint of rocky road ice cream. I was about to hang out with my algebra book and try not to think about what a loser I was. I concluded that, at least for me, being an adult stank.

Chapter Fourteen

After dancing solo all weekend, I was eager for the distraction that work brought on Monday so I wouldn't have to focus on what a no-fun loser I had become. The weather must have decided to match my mood, and a low sheet of endless gray clouds moved in, warning of snow. Wrapping my jacket tighter around my body, I walked faster, relieved when I got to duck into the warmth of the store.

"Do you ever sleep?" I asked Gabby, who sat at her desk with stacks of fabric samples fanned out in front of her, looking like she was hours into her project already.

"Not much." She held up a black corduroy square. "What do think of this one for a coat? Maybe with a gold plaid lining?"

Scrunching my nose, I tried to visualize myself wearing something like that. It would be too bulky for my style. "It looks sort of masculine. It would be fine if that's what you're going for."

Dropping the fabric back onto her desk, she sat back with her feet stretched long in front of her. "I don't know what I'm going for." Her eyes drifted to the front door as the first of the construction crew arrived for the day. Then she leaned over and quietly asked, "Has Jesse ever talked to you?"

"Huh?" I said as I stood by her desk and helped myself to her fabric samples, sorting them by colors.

She let her eyes lead me to a guy in the back of the store, fastening his tool belt. "Jesse," she whispered. "Has he ever talked to you?"

"No, why?" I spotted a tan suede fabric sample peeking out from the bottom of her pile. "Oh, this is what you're looking for." I grabbed it and held it out for her. "This with a gold lining and maybe a soft fur trim." I caressed it against my cheek. "I love it."

"I noticed he smiles at you a lot." She pursed her lips out, ignoring my fabric swatch. "He's not much older than you, you know."

I snorted. "The last thing I need is a construction guy."

She gave me a quizzical look. "You don't think he's cute?"

"Who are you?" I flipped my hand out in a questioning gesture. "What did you do to my workaholic boss?"

She laughed, letting her eyes retreat to her own project. "Sorry, didn't mean to pry."

Now, I was curious, so I casually set the fabric back down, sneaking a peek over my shoulder at him. I didn't try to notice but it was pretty hard not to. He had the physique that could land him on the cover of a construction guy calendar. *He was cute.* Then I sighed—like I was being tossed into a dreamland where dating was easy—before letting my eyes land back on my pile of work on my desk, and I declared, "I don't have time for a personal life."

"I know what you mean." She leaned over her desk calendar then looked back over her shoulder out the window. "Oh, my interviewee must be here." She pointed outside to a petite woman with a trendy, sleek bob, and oversized sunglasses.

I watched as the woman peeked through the window and then tried the door, letting herself in. I jumped up to greet her. "Hi."

Her ruby lips curled upward, greeting me back, "Hi, I'm Lexi, and I have an appointment with Gabby."

"That's me." Gabby walked over and shook her hand. "Nice to meet you."

"Nice to meet you too," Lexi replied, her voice showcased her southern accent.

"It's pretty noisy in here." Gabby motioned toward the construction mess. "Why don't we run across the street to that café to chat?" She flung her purse over her shoulder and ushered Lexi out the door.

I watched them cross the street, wondering if she would be our new coworker. Unable to focus on work because I was nervous, hoping Gabby was pleased with my recommendation, I nervously checked my phone and found a text.

Fulton: *Sorry about your birthday. I'm feeling better. Would you want to come to Wednesday comedy club?*

I exhaled heavily. I had been looking forward to having *alone* time with Fulton over dinner. Comedy club would be more of the same. I wouldn't get to talk to him because of Candace. I enjoyed watching Wally because he made me laugh, but I wanted to say no and tell him I would rather do something with the two of us, but I also didn't want to come off as possessive like Candace.

Me: *Yeah, I'd love to!*

Just when I looked up from my phone, a couple of the construction workers walked past my desk on their way outside.

One of them was Jesse, who smiled at me. I was pretty sure it wasn't an accident, but it caught me off guard. My mouth dropped open as I stared back at him, and I forgot how to be human. *Smile!* I yelled at myself, but I don't think my lips worked the way they were supposed to. He left, then I remembered to close my mouth. I wanted to scream away the embarrassment, but I didn't want him to hear me. Socializing used to be easy for me, but this was excruciating. Disgusted with myself, I hung my head over my invoices and vowed to get it right the next time.

After an hour, Gabby returned by herself, quick to get back on her computer with an all-business look on her face. "How'd it go?" I asked, knowing I was interrupting her, but I was feeling the need to converse with someone.

"I'm not sure." She tilted her head, thoughtfully. "She did great with the interview, but I can tell she's polished from years of management. She knows what the best answers to my questions are, so I'm not sure if she actually believes them or if she just knows the right things to say."

"What kind of a vibe did you get?"

"Not really any yet."

"Well, hopefully the next one goes better."

She refreshed the sales screen and after she finished reviewing it, she stretched her legs out long beneath her desk, and leaned back, coolly crossing her arms over her chest, "Anything happen here?"

"I tried to smile at Jesse, but apparently I suck at flirting."

She chuckled, like she was letting out decades of dating failures. "Welcome to the club. I haven't figured it out yet, and I'm over forty." She reached into her purse and pulled out the bag of mixed chocolates. "Here, go ahead and medicate."

I wasn't going to say no to chocolate, so I generously dumped a whole handful of candy out before handing it back to her. "Do you ever date?" I asked curiously.

"Let's see." She popped a few candies in her mouth while she thought. "I think I've been on four dates since I moved here twenty years ago." She stared blankly at the wall, and added, "It's hard. Easier to work."

"Four." I felt my eyebrows lift in disbelief. "Why so few?"

"I'm bad at dating."

"Don't you ever get lonely?"

"I don't because I have so much work to do. I think that's my issue. I created a life with zero work-life balance."

Not wanting to pry anymore, I let my eyes fall to my hands, and I nervously picked at my nails. I was grateful for my job, but I desperately didn't want to end up alone like her. I didn't like having no one to hang out with on my birthday. I needed people. Even when I was on the farm, I at least had Fulton's little sister, Millie, to hang out with when I was bored. Here, I felt like I was wasting my life.

Gabby must have sensed my confliction because she spoke up. "What about that roach guy? He was super cute."

"Wally?" I quickly shook my head. "He flirts with anything that has a pulse."

Her face remained indifferent. "So then that other guy who was here. The tall one?" Her question pelted right to the center of my heart, causing a constriction. When I didn't answer her, she smiled knowingly and dropped the bag of chocolate back on my desk. "You need this more than I do."

"It sucks." I lowered my eyes again, stuffed another piece of candy into my mouth, surprised that I had basically admitted to my boss that I liked Fulton.

"He was with that girl, right?" Her eyes were wide.

I rolled my eyes. "He says he's not *with* her. They're just friends, but he's never not with her."

Then I held my eyes in communion with hers, waiting for her to give me advice, to tell me what to do, but she didn't say anything more about him. Her next interview arrived, and they went to the café. I managed to go through the motions of work, but my mind was churning like it was coming out of a long fog—finally able to clearly see the objects that had been blurry. Now that I had admitted it and said the words out loud, I couldn't deny my feelings any longer. My thoughts rushed, making my cheeks burn like wildfire, but at the same time, my confusion over the mixed signals and Candace always being around still prodded my heart enough to make my knees weak in doubt.

I tried to let my thoughts get lost in my invoices, but I was so distracted by the way my heart kept racing every time I thought about Fulton. Finally giving up, I gathered my things ready to call it day. With my mind in the clouds, I let myself out of the store, ready to walk home, when I had to stop hard on my heels, because I had totally spaced that I needed to lock up since Gabby had already left. I dug in my purse for my keys and muttered, *"Get a grip, Abs."* I was total mess when I stuck my key in the lock, my hands were even jittery. Feeling my heart was fully on loan at this point. As much as it scared me to say anything to him, I had to believe that he had similar feelings and at this point, I just didn't see why I was avoiding my feelings anymore. So, while I walked home that night,

I pledged that the next time I saw Fulton, I would talk to him about what I had been feeling.

Chapter Fifteen

Wednesday rolled around, and you would have thought I was getting ready for the prom. I changed clothes three times and reapplied my lip gloss at least as many times as I looked at the clock. I had met up with him hundreds of times in my life, and I had never once before obsessed over what I looked like. Not wanting to be early because I didn't want to look eager, but I also didn't want to be late because that would give him the impression I didn't care. Anxious thoughts raced through my head. When I rechecked my phone again to make sure the numbers didn't move, it rang.

Seeing it was my dad, I quickly answered. "Hey, Dad."

"Hey, are you busy?"

"No, I'm waiting until it's time to leave to go to comedy club." I paced my room like I had consumed half a dozen energy drinks and was now locked in a cage.

"Do you have a few minutes, or should I call back?" His voice was tense, worried.

I froze. "I have time."

"Well, I'm concerned. I don't want to be harsh on you because I know you're working hard. Gabby has told me several times about how hard you're working."

"But . . ." I held my breath.

"I got your report card. You're failing two classes and have a D in the other two."

I exhaled but didn't speak.

"I know I don't need to remind you what the deal was," he continued. "I only let you take that internship on the terms that you kept up with your high school. School is the priority. If you're failing school, I'm going to ask you to not go back to work."

"What? You can't do that," I spit out. "Gabby needs me."

"I can. Gabby knows you need to finish school. If you can't do both, then the job needs to go away."

"What's the point of school though?" I argued. "I'm not learning anything I'll ever use. I learn way better when I actually do something instead of reading it in a book."

"The point is that you need to finish."

"I can drop out. I'm eighteen."

"Don't play that card. You're not dropping out."

"Why not?"

"Because. What are you going to do when you drop out? I'm not paying rent for a high-school dropout. If you drop out, you're on your own." His voice raised in volume but still held more concern than anger. "Your job with Gabby is unpaid. You're not going to get far with a job that doesn't pay you, no place to live, and no high school education. I'm paying for this experience, so I'm the boss. You have until Christmas break to pass all your classes, or you are coming home."

I swallowed. I loathed school. I always felt so stupid when I poured my heart into studying, and then I would get my exams back with a terrible grade marked in red ink at the top. I was never a book-smart person. When I was in regular school, I used my popularity to offset how bad failure made me feel, but I wasn't popular anymore. I had no friends. I had nothing. Nothing but stupid online school I couldn't even pass. He was right. I was stuck. And I had to play by his rules. I had to get my grades up because going home was not an option. "I'm sorry. I know you trusted me. It wasn't that I haven't tried, but I'll try harder," I said.

"Good. I know you can do this. You deserve this for yourself." The word *deserve* echoed. What I deserved? I deserved to be able to live in my house with a mom who loved me. I never pretended for a second this move was all about me. I knew from day one it had as much to do with my mom and her need for space as it did for me to get work experience and a break from the farm. My dad needed me gone as much as I needed to be gone. It was never about what I deserved.

I licked my lips to try to make my words come out easier. "I know. I'm sorry. I'll do better."

"I know you will. I'll let you go so you can get on with your night."

"Bye." I ended the call and clutched my phone to my chest, wondering how the person who was supposed to take care of me could also be the same person that needed me to stay away.

My mood had plummeted, and I sulked while I walked to the theatre. The thing my dad didn't understand was I had been trying with school. Online school was a lot harder than regular school in so many ways, particularly because you have no interaction with the teacher. Plus, you have to find the time to do it, whereas with regular school you're there all day so you might as well participate.

By the time I spotted the group at the VIP table, I had lost interest in being out. My negative feelings only multiplied when I sat down in the last empty seat on the edge of the table. I was right next to Wally and diagonally across from Fulton on a longer table, so it was hard to even try to talk to Fulton.

"How's it going?" Fulton raised his voice to ask over the table noise.

"Alright."

"You look stressed."

That's the thing about Fulton. I loved how he was good at reading people, but when he used his superpower against me, it was annoying. "It's nothing," I dismissed, not wanting to get into my personal life in front of his friends. A conversation about football was getting heated between Griz and Wally, and I pretended to care.

"I can't believe you got him to come out." I motioned to Griz. "I've never seen him here."

"He's always worked Wednesday nights, but he got a promotion, so his hours changed," Fulton explained.

"Oh." I was about to start a conversation back with him, but then Wally leaned in, giving me a friendly elbow. "What's up, Aubergine?" Dressed up with a black button shirt, gray suspenders and a matching felt fedora, he looked pretty spiffy compared to everyone else who sported their casual collegiate t-shirts.

"Not much," I replied, and offered a compliment, "Nice hat. It's very classy." I reached out to feel it. "And nice fabric too. Is this part of the show tonight?"

"No, I'm not performing tonight."

"You're not. How come?"

"I'm taking over a slot on Saturdays now. It's a bigger audience. Wednesday is more of a college night, and we had more comedians who wanted to try it, so I moved up."

"That's cool. Congrats on the new show," I said.

"Thanks. I dressed up because now that I don't perform on Wednesdays, I'm helping my dad, and I'm the manager on duty."

While he talked, my eyes shifted back to the others at the table. College football was still the main topic being tossed around, but something about Fulton looked different; he was slouched in his chair when he normally had great posture. Not surprisingly, Candace's posture matched Fulton's, and she had slouched way down too. I could feel my eyebrow fold inward when I noticed what was different—Fulton had his arm around her! It shouldn't have shocked me because they were always together, but Fulton always insisted they were only friends. Up until now, I had never seen him reciprocate any affection toward her.

"You okay?" Wally asked. "You look sort of flushed."

"Yea—" I started to say I was fine, but there was no point in pretending. I had come here to see Fulton. He obviously had different ideas than I did. I can't pretend to be fine while Fulton cuddled with Candace. "No, I'm not okay. I think I'm coming down with something."

"Do you want to get some air?" The look of concern on his face was growing, and I was now panicking to get out of the room before other people noticed I wasn't okay. I didn't say anything but twisted, looking for the exit door.

"Or do you want me to get a ride home for you?" Wally suggested.

I glanced at Fulton, worried he would overhear Wally's concern for me, but Fulton was deep into football analytics that were over my head. I needed time to digest Fulton's new situation alone, so I didn't make a scene. "You know, I'm not going to stay for the show, but I'll be okay getting home by myself." I stood, trying to be quiet so Fulton wouldn't notice I was leaving. I slipped away, before he called after me, and before I knew it, I was half-sprinting outside. I didn't stop until I reached the street corner, where the no-crossing sign was flashing. I skidded to a stop right when it turned red.

"Just wait. I can walk you home in case you get sick." Wally called from somewhere behind me,

"Nah, I'm fine to walk." I glared at the crossing light, desperately wishing it would turn green already.

"I know why you're sick."

I turned to see him standing inches from me. His brown eyes pried. "Oh," I said flatly.

"They were fighting all last week about your birthday."

The light turned green, but my stupid feet didn't walk. My spine straightened, and I just had to take the bait and ask, "My birthday?"

"Candace didn't want him to take you to dinner."

My brow lowered and I insisted, "He was sick last week." I could see the patience in his eyes while he waited for me to understand. "He wasn't sick?" I asked.

He barely nodded his head to confirm Fulton had lied to me.

My brain told me to just walk away and that it wasn't worth the heartache, but my stupid fallible heart needed to hear what was next. So, I pressed, "Why are you telling me this?"

He shrugged, locking his eyes on mine. "I thought you should know."

"So, are they together now?"

"From what I know, he told her that he wasn't ready to commit, but she was emotional and wouldn't drop it, so he said they could try."

I chewed my lip, not wanting to comment because I wasn't supposed to care what Fulton did in his personal life. Then a miracle happened, and the light changed to green again. I pointed to it. "I have to go."

I took a step off the curb, but he called after me, "It's not going to last."

One foot hovered on the curb while my other foot anchored me on the street. Go home, I yelled at myself, but instead I turned back. "You don't think so?" I waited for him to tell me what to do, but he didn't say anything else, so I filled in the silence, "This stinks."

His lips curved up slightly, as he reached his hand out to me. "Come on. I'll show you somewhere we can hide and throw popcorn at them."

Twisting my lips in a curious manner, I wondered if he was serious. Then before I knew what I was doing I begrudgingly moved toward him, and we started to walk back toward the theatre together. I looked at him and said, "Throwing popcorn? That sounds mature."

Then he gave me his mischievous grin. "Let's be honest. Neither one of us really wants to act mature right now."

The laugh that escaped my lips was more of a snort than I cared to own, but it did help me to feel better. Then continuing to follow him back inside, I pondered where he was taking me. If I was being honest, I mostly followed him because I really did want to throw stuff at Candace.

Chapter Sixteen

"I used to hide up here when I was little to sneak into the adult shows." Wally led me up a narrow flight of steps and into a cramped room. "This is the old projector room. The glass on the window is tinted. We can see out, but no one can see you. Plus," he said as he opened the little door, revealing a window designed for the projector. "It's perfect to spill stuff on people."

"Why am I not surprised?" I wagged my head. "Who did you throw stuff at?"

"Yes, I know it's shocking to some, but I've not always been this mature." He tipped his fedora at me.

I walked close to the door but didn't look over the ledge. "Who'd you target?"

He lowered himself onto a chair. "Well, my first crush, Amy Sandori, came here with the most popular guy in the seventh grade, and it totally destroyed me."

"That's why they call it a crush."

"True story."

"Did she see you?"

"Amy never saw me ever. Not in school. Not here. I sat up here and hurled popcorn at their heads for at least a half an hour before they got up and moved. It was vindicating." Holding his popcorn bucket out to me, he gave it a shake and urged, "You go first."

I grinned, slyly. "Yeah, right."

He shook the bucket again. "I'm serious. Go ahead. One shot. You'll feel so much better."

"I can't throw popcorn at them."

"Why not? You can't get in trouble. I'm the manager, and I didn't see anything." His mischievous grin was back. Not only did I find it oddly comforting but it also made me want to play along.

"One shot." I matched his smile with my own devious expression as I selected one perfect piece of popped corn. Then I crouched down on the floor under the window and stretched my neck over the ledge to locate them. They were still cozied up, enjoying the show. Adjusting my aim for perfect pitch, I then hurled the kernel and watched it bounce off Candace's shoulder before it hit the floor. I quickly ducked down.

"She can't see you," Wally reminded me when he crouched next to me, positioning himself for battle.

"I still feel like I need to hide."

"It does make it more fun," he affirmed. "My turn." He rose, carefully studying his target. I peeked over the ledge when he threw his kernel. It arched perfectly, landing smack in the middle of Candace's head. I slid down with my back against the wall, stifling my giggle.

He hid next to me, eyes full of humor. "You feel better, right?"

"Totally."

He extended the bucket out toward me. "One more?"

"Nah, I think I'm good. One was enough for me."

"Want to watch the show?"

Having been so wrapped up in my emotions, I hadn't realized there was a comedian onstage. The audience looked engaged, but I didn't feel into it anymore. "Not really."

"You want to go home, don't you?"

"I do."

"I get it." With that, he stood, leading the way out of the darkened room and down the hall. I walked slowly, noticing the wall lined in framed photographs of entertainers. Most of them were black and white and no one I recognized. "I love how when they posed in the old days, they always looked so proper," I said when I pointed to a photograph of a woman sitting with perfect posture on a stool. Her legs were crossed, aimed toward the camera to show off the ruffles on the bottom of her dress cut a few inches above her ankles.

"I love that photo. It's from the nineteen twenties, the first year the theatre was opened."

"This theatre has been here forever."

"It's a landmark, and it's been in my family the whole time. I'll be the fourth-generation owner."

"That's amazing." I let my finger linger back over the picture. "I love the style of the dress. So feminine. You can tell they knew how to sew too. Look at all those layers. And the fabric was so rich."

He leaned his side against the wall, watching me closely, and then said, "I feel like if I don't pull you away from that picture now, I'll have to scrub it for drool."

"I'm not that bad." I made sure my mouth was closed. Then I browsed the next photograph on the wall. A woman stood on the theatre stage, which looked exactly how it was today down to the red velvet curtains and gold tassels. "Your family has done a phenomenal job of keeping the theatre in its original design," I complimented.

"I couldn't imagine it any other way. For a while, people thought it looked dated, and everyone else had long moved to modern theatres and technology. The traditional style is what attracts people to us now. I hope to always keep it like a time capsule to the past."

The woman in the photograph drew my eyes back to her with her dress devoid of curves yet draped in beads. "Look at her. She's ravishing."

"That's my nana."

"You're kidding."

"She was a singer and one of the reasons her dad opened the theatre. Believe it or not, her dress was considered scandalous back then. People refused to come hear her sing because of the way her dress was just below the knees."

"And now, it seems rather modest compared to what I see every day in high fashion."

"Right?" he agreed.

I looked back at her picture and saw she was expressionless. "You know, when I look at this dress, it makes me want to see her face. Like, her dress is so beautiful, I'm expecting the most beautiful face. Do you know what I mean?"

"Maybe a little. All these photographs up here are intriguing, and they make me want to know the people in them." He flipped a light switch on the wall, illuminating the rest of the hallway and revealing hundreds of more photographs. Each photograph was autographed before it was framed and hung in chronological order of time. Wally continued, "The twenties were a time when everything rose; skyscrapers rose from the ground, the stock market rose way up, and woman's skirts kept going way up too. It had to have been magical."

"I'm sure the men thought woman's skirts rising was magical," I teased him.

"Well, yeah, I bet that was." He chuckled. "But I think it all had to be. It was a time when success was easy."

I tilted my head back, taking in the collage of photos, letting my eyes linger on each one long enough so I would notice their facial expressions and their clothes. "Your hallway is like a museum."

"It should be one day when the time is right. But for now, we keep it as our own treasure. It was my great-grandfather who started the collection with that picture of his daughter. She was the first performer on this stage, and he continued the tradition after that."

"I can honestly say I've never been more impressed by a wall."

"We like it too." He lowered his eyes thoughtfully, then lifted them to meet mine. "And if you ever decide to take me up on my offer to dance here, then you'll get to hang among all these entertainers."

"What an honor that would be," I said out loud, but I meant it more for myself.

"You can stay here all night if it makes you happy, but if you're ready to go, I can walk you home."

My eyes micro focused on Nana and her timeless beauty, absorbing it all and filing it into my memory. Then I slowly turned away, joining Wally at his side. "Yeah, I'm ready to go home, but thanks for sharing this with me."

"You're welcome. Wait until I show you backstage." His grin was wide across his face. "That'll explode your mind."

I followed him down the stairs and said, "I don't know if I can handle something of that caliber."

"I'll save it for when we need something drastic to cheer you up. Like Fulton and Candace's wedding."

"Ha!" I blurted out. "If that ever happens, I'm going to need to be flown to the moon."

Chapter Seventeen

The following week, I was surprised to see a new face with us. "Let's sit down together for a few minutes so we can get to know Lexi," Gabby said as she relaxed on her chair next to her new employee, Lexi, who wore on-trend glasses. Her dark hair was tied back in a ponytail so short that it looked like a stub.

Scooting my chair over to join them, I leaned forward to greet her, "How's your morning going?"

"It's good. I'm excited to be here."

"You're going to love working for Gabby. We never have a dull moment," I said.

Gabby smiled at me like we shared a secret. "It can get crazy, but the cool thing is we always get along."

"We do," I agreed, "but that might be because I'm scared of you."

"Ha!" Gabby threw her head back in laughter. "If you're scared of me, then you're in for a long life."

"I'm kidding." I returned my gaze back to Lexi. "Gabby's great, and we do get along well."

"That's important to me," Gabby said. "I hear these horror stories from my friends about the drama they have at work, and I hope we never have that. That's one of the things you said in your interview that made me like you. You said you try hard to facilitate a fun environment."

"I do," Lexi picked up the conversation. "I think everyone can work hard, but since we spend more of our lives at work than anywhere else, I want to enjoy it."

"I think we'll all get along well." Gabby eyed each of us individually. "This first week might feel insane for you, but don't hesitate to ask me or Abs if any questions come up."

"I'm sure I'll be full of questions once I start to get orientated," Lexi said.

Gabby looked at me. "Lexi's going to work with me this week, mostly helping to oversee the store production, and we'll start screening applicants to bring on the rest of our sales team. We won't be open by Black Friday, but I'm okay with that. We'll be a little late to the party and open the first weekend in December."

"That would be good because we can hire everyone in the next two weeks and start training right after Thanksgiving," Lexi said, and then added, "Nobody wants to start a new job right before Thanksgiving,"

"I agree," Gabby said. "So, we'll all be off for Thanksgiving, and I don't mind if you want to take Friday off too." She looked at both of us again. "You might be able to get some good shopping in or relax to get ready for our big push that will start the following week."

"That sounds doable," I said. "Do you want me on freight today?"

She gave me a warning look. "Actually, this is the last day we have access to the old studio. Everything's been moved, but we need to clean."

"Are the roaches gone?" I asked while gritting my teeth.

"It's been sprayed, and the hole's been sealed. If you wouldn't mind, can you spend the time over there to get it ready so I can turn in my keys?"

"I can." I reluctantly nodded, realizing my job got less glamorous every day.

"Thank you." Gabby held her clipboard, flipped up the top page, browsing the sheets. "That's all I have for today." She returned her look toward me. "You can go ahead and ship out. When you're done over there, you can go home for the day, even if you finish early."

"Deal." I hurriedly gathered my things before Gabby gave me more work assignments and headed for the door. Just as I was about to push the door open, Jesse walked up from the outside, opening the door for me. Walking forward, I started to feel a little tense, but turned to him and somehow managed to smile at him this time when he said, "Hi."

I said, "Thank you," and walked by. Proud that I didn't look like a complete dork again, my smile grew as I made my way to the studio. Then my phone rang, and I took a quick look at the caller I.D., but that made my mood instantly tank again. I didn't want to answer it, but I did anyway.

"Hey," I said.

"Are you feeling better?" Fulton's concerned voice came across my phone.

"Huh?"

"From last night. Didn't you get sick?"

I had forgotten I had used that excuse to leave, but even then, I was sure he hadn't seen me leave. "How'd you know?"

"I noticed you had left, so I was worried about what happened. Then Wally came home and mentioned he had walked you home because you had gotten sick. Did you eat something that didn't agree with you?"

"I don't think I even ate last night," I said, truthfully.

"That might have been the problem. Maybe you had low blood sugar or something," he wondered out loud.

"Maybe. I feel fine now."

"Good. Are you still at work?"

"Technically yes, but not in the store. I'm on my way to go clean out the studio. Why do you ask?"

"Just wondering."

I waited for him to break the silence, wondering if he'd bring up Candace, but instead, he said, "Do you have plans for the holiday weekend?"

"I'm off work for four days, so I'm excited to not work. I'm going to sleep, do laundry, and, unfortunately, I need to catch up on my algebra. What about you?"

"We are going to comedy club on Wednesday still, even though Wally isn't performing. It's like a habit we can't break. Do you want to come again?"

Part of me wanted to ask why he even bothered asking me when he hardly talked to me. If it hadn't been for Wally having pity on me last night, I would have been completely humiliated sitting all alone. "I don't know—" I started but Fulton talked over me.

"Sorry I didn't notice you leave last night. I barely got to talk to you. I'll try to get there earlier to save you a closer seat. It was so crowded last night, and you were so far away I sort of forgot you were there." The tone of his voice was apologetic, but I could tell he wasn't apologizing for not saving me a seat. Something awkward was happening between us since he now had a girlfriend. He felt it as much as I did, but neither one of us knew what to do about it.

"No biggie." I tried to sound neutral, surprised by how much this conversation was upsetting me.

"So, I'll save you a seat next Wednesday?" he asked slowly.

I took a deep breath, scolding myself for being a pushover. "Sure."

"Great. I'll see you then."

"Okay, bye." I ended the call, telling myself if next week was awkward, then that'd be the last time I'd try to be friends with him. It stunk though, because even before I had admitted I had a crush on him, I didn't have anyone else to hang out with. If Fulton ditches me again, I'll just have to get good at smiling at Jesse.

I swung into the corner drug store for a quick stop, knowing the drug store closed early. Since I wasn't sure how long cleaning would take, I wanted to make sure I had cash. Making a mental list of all the things I needed to replenish at my dorm, I punched in my pin, but my card was declined. I tried it again, but the same message came up saying I had insufficient funds.

I pulled out my phone and pressed send on my dad's name. "Hey," I said when he answered.

"Hey hon, how's it going?"

"Ah, something's weird." I stared at my debit card. "I went to get cash and the machine declined me, saying I didn't have the money. Did you put money in my account?"

"I did," he replied. "Are you tracking your spending? Because you should have more than enough for the month."

"What do you mean by tracking my spending?"

"I mean, do you write down what you are taking out to make sure you are staying in your budget?"

I didn't even know what he meant by budget. He had always put money in my account when I needed it. My silence must have answered his question.

"Do you remember when I said I would pay your rent so you didn't have to worry about that, and I would put money in your account for necessities, but you would have to budget that to last for the month?"

"I remember you telling me that, but I thought you meant you would give me money to pay for everything. I didn't think I had to write it down."

"Not just write it down. Keep track of what you're spending and think about the expenses you have coming up. It's called budgeting. Do you really have no idea how to do that?"

"I've heard about it, but I didn't think I'd have to do it."

"Yes, this is part of the learning experience for you. I want you to learn how to do this, so you know how when you're on your own. I'm not giving you unlimited funds."

"Well, when do I get more money?"

"The first of the month like always."

"That's a week away."

"Yes, it is."

"You're not going to give me any money until then?"

"Do you have any food at your place?"

I thought about the half-empty boxes of snack food I had stashed in my cupboard for my late-night study sessions and my stacks of Thai noodles. "Not enough to last a week."

I heard him expel a sigh. "I'll transfer fifty dollars. That's enough for you to get the essentials to eat on for the week, but you'll have to do a budget."

"Only fifty? I spend that in a day on coffee and food. Plus, I have to buy clothes for work."

"I know you do. That's why you ran out of money. But you need to practice living on less. You're three months into this internship, and it won't last forever. Then you'll be on your own, and I promise you, any starting salary you get is going to be a cut in your lifestyle."

I wondered how much of a cut someone could take after they were used to living off-grid, but I didn't want to challenge him. "Okay, thanks. I appreciate your help," I said.

"You're welcome. You can do this," he said.

"I'll try. Bye." I ended the call, knowing I *would* do this because it was my only option, but I didn't want to. I put my debit card and my phone back into my purse and left the store, thinking that it would be one depressing Thanksgiving.

Chapter Eighteen

It hurt to spend my last ten dollars chasing a boy who didn't think about me the way I thought about him. I also knew I had four days off from work, and if I didn't get out of my dorm a little, I would probably go stir crazy, especially since all my shopping plans for Black Friday had been thwarted due to my new budget.

I did my best to buy food to come in under budget. I had money left over to go to comedy club on Wednesday, but a tiny miracle happened that night. I could feel my face light up when I saw Wally taking tickets at the door. "You can just go in," he waved me through the door without taking my money.

I clenched my ten-dollar bill like it was a golden egg. "Thank you."

"You're welcome. I'll be in as soon as the door closes."

"See you in a bit." I took my time strolling through the hall, studying the old photos. The image of Nana's dress had stayed with me all week. I managed to spot a couple of photos by the bathrooms that pacified my fashion curiosity too. Both photos displayed women dressed in long coats and heels, but the thing that stuck out to me was their hats. They were round and fit like an upside-down bowl with a feather placed in the middle, adding a delicate touch. Both of their coats also had feminine adornments on them, one with fur trim and the other lace. The way the woman stood mimicked the way the clothes looked, dainty and feminine. I was mesmerized.

"You're not working tonight?" a voice asked from behind me.

I pivoted to see the voice was coming from an elderly man dressed in a long wool coat and matching hat. It took me a minute to recognize him as Wally's father. "Oh no." I shook my head. "I'm joining friends."

"I knew you didn't work here. I was teasing." His smile was easy and a mirror image of Wally's natural glimmer, like his face didn't know how to have any other expressions.

"Are you watching the show tonight?" I asked, making small talk.

"I watch the show every night. That's what I do. And I hold my wife's purse while she uses the ladies' room." He held up a red leather bag to illustrate his point. "Those are the two things I do." The bag was studded with great hardware, and I could tell the leather was genuine.

"That's a great bag." I motioned to it.

"Like I always say, if I have to hold a lady's purse, it might as well be one that makes me look fashionable."

"You always say that?" I smiled cautiously.

"No." He shook his head. "I've never said that. I made that up." He laughed until I joined him in his joy. His wife appeared from the bathroom, dressed equally classy.

"Is he troubling you?" she asked me.

"No, not at all. We're just chatting about handbags."

"Handbags? I dare say Henry knows little about handbags." She looped her bag through her wrist.

"Not true, dear. I know the good ones make my pockets lighter but are always heavier for me to hold."

I smiled at his wit. I was about to excuse myself to find our table when Wally walked up from the side and joined in. "Do I dare ask what you're talking about?"

His dad gave Wally his easy grin. "Purses."

"I don't even want to know." Wally rolled his eyes. "You'd better grab a seat. It's time for the show."

"He's right," Henry said to his wife, and he held out his arm for her to hold.

"Okay." She joined him but her gorgeous blue eyes peered toward Wally. "Thanksgiving is tomorrow. Nana has been missing you. Are you coming for lunch or dinner?"

"I hadn't thought about it, but I'll probably want to sleep in, so maybe nothing too early."

"How about four o'clock?"

"That's fine," Wally agreed.

Wally's mom started to walk away, but his dad looked back and said, "You can bring the pretty one if you want." He motioned to me.

"I'm sure she has plans," Wally quickly replied with an air of annoyance in his voice. He waited in silence until they were gone. "We can go in if you're ready, or are you waiting for the bathroom?"

"No, I'm not waiting. I was admiring your photos when your mom came out."

"Ah, man, did you drool on them again?" He dramatically leaned over to examine them.

I chuckled. "Almost. I can't get over their fashion."

His eyes did a final wave across the photos. "It must be a girl thing, because I don't see it."

I shrugged. "Maybe."

"So, are we joining the love birds at the table tonight or throwing stuff at them from the projector room again?" He gave me one of those looks that said he was up for anything.

"We can sit with them. I'm over it."

"Alright then. You can stick with me so you don't have to look at them." We moved through the auditorium and he continued the conversation in a hushed voice. "Sorry about my parents. They are overly involved in my life. You know how it is, always trying to pry into everything."

I lowered my eyebrows. "I didn't get that from them at all. I thought they were cute."

"How was that cute?"

"How wasn't it cute? Your dad stood near the lady's restroom and held your mom's purse like a total gentleman, and he did it with pride. Very chivalrous."

"Don't let him fool you," Wally said through strained lips.

"He even invited me to dinner. How charitable is that?"

"It's nosey. They always invite my friends over so they can eavesdrop on our conversations." Wally pulled up one of the chairs at the table for himself and left the empty seat next to Fulton for me.

"I was beginning to think you weren't going to come," Fulton said to me after I sat.

"I was talking to Wally's parents in the hall."

Fulton raised an eyebrow toward Wally, who rolled his eyes. "Oh, they're interesting, aren't they?"

"I thought they were cute," I said.

"They invited her to dinner tomorrow, and now she thinks they are cute," Wally explained to Fulton.

"Are you going to go?" Fulton asked me.

"Go where?" I asked.

"To Wally's."

"Oh no, I don't think I was invited for real." My eyes darted to Wally. "Was I?"

He held up his hand like he was giving up. "Sure, why not?"

"It's okay," I said. "I don't even know your parents. Your dad was teasing. I'll be doing my algebra all day tomorrow." I made a face like I had just learned I needed a root canal.

"You don't have anywhere to go?" Fulton asked.

I felt like he was putting me on the spot unnecessarily when it should have been obvious to him that I didn't have any family in town anymore. "No, do you?" I asked defensively.

"He's coming with me upstate to my folk's house," Candace answered for him.

"Oh," I managed. Then, when I couldn't think of anything else to say, I finally added, "Well, have fun with that," but it came out with a hint of sarcasm. I immediately felt bad and bit my lip even though the only person who appeared to notice my comment was Wally. His smile spread wide across his face as he shook his head at me.

I leaned my head back. *I was never going to be okay sitting next to Fulton while he made plans to meet his new girlfriend's parents.*

I regretted coming, and I told myself I would be happy for him from a distance after tonight. The lights dimmed and the show started. I was glad to have the attention taken off me not having Thanksgiving plans, but Wally must have felt sorry for me because he wouldn't drop it.

"If you want to come to my house, my parents would be happy to see you," he whispered. "They love interrogating new people."

"No," I whispered back. "It's fine. Really. I need to do my math."

"Don't you have all weekend to do it?"

"Shh." Someone from across the aisle made a face at Wally.

I looked straight ahead and vowed not to talk, but Wally persisted. "Meet me at Penn Station at ten o'clock."

I shook my head.

"Seriously, if you're not there," he continued in a hushed voice, "I'll come to your apartment."

I looked over at him, prepared to give him an unappreciative glare, but my face froze when I saw his eyes were wide and sincere. Leaning close to his ear to conceal the conversation, I whispered, "It's really not a big deal. I'm used to being by myself."

"Just come for fun. It won't be too bad. You can hang out with me and practice being fun Abs."

"I am fun."

"If you don't say yes right now, I'll start screaming that you smell bad." His mischievous grin dared me.

I leaned over again and tried to keep my voice quiet. "I don't even know your parents. It would be awkward."

He pinched his nose closed with his fingers and started to look around. "What's that smell?" he asked in a loud voice.

I grabbed his hand, yanking it down. "Stop it." I urged. "Shh."

"Say it."

"Fine," I whispered. "I'll come."

"Was that so hard?"

"Sort of." I slouched in my chair, completely embarrassed even though no one seemed to care, especially not Fulton who was cuddling with Candace. I focused on the show and counted down the minutes until I got to go home.

Chapter Nineteen

On Thanksgiving afternoon, I took the trip with Wally to his parent's house on Long Island. We stepped off the train in Manhasset, and Wally motioned down the street. "It's a ten-minute walk this way."

"What are you, old money?" I asked when I saw his neighborhood, knowing the area because I had been to a birthday party in elementary school for one of my classmates. My dad had done some marketing for her parents who were in finance, but my dad said most of their wealth had been "old money." I looked self-consciously at the bouquet of filler flowers I had gotten from the street stand to give to Wally's mom. Had I known this was his neighborhood, I would have cleaned out my pockets to round up another few bucks in change to spring for a bouquet with a lily or even a few carnations in it.

"Everything about my parents is old," Wally replied. "If you haven't noticed, they're, like, a hundred." It sounded like he wanted to vent about his parents. I didn't want to say anything bad about his folks because they had been nice to me. I focused on what a gorgeous day it was with birds scattered on the sidewalks, and the sun peeking out of the clouds with a promise to shine even brighter. We walked and I watched the houses get bigger and the bushes get taller until we reached a street with gated yards.

Wally said, "I'm sure you're good at reading people, but my parents can be pretty stubborn in their views. It's best to not talk about certain things."

"I get it."

"Okay, I'm just warning you."

"How old are your parents?"

"They're in their late sixties, going on a hundred."

"You must have been the baby in the family."

"Yeah, my mom couldn't get pregnant, so they never had kids. Instead, they had the theatre. Then my mom ended up getting surprised with a pregnancy in her late forties."

"I bet you were totally spoiled."

"I don't think I was. I was mostly left with a nanny."

"That's interesting. Were you always the funny kid?"

"Actually, no. I used to be shy and quiet. Then one night, the nanny never showed up, and my dad had to take me to the theatre while he worked. I hid upstairs in that projector room and there was this comedian on stage. I had never seen anything like it, and then, just like that, there was a switch that went off in my head. I knew that's what I wanted to do."

"Really? I would have thought it was natural."

"I've been studying it since I was five, so I hope I learned something." He rounded the corner and walked into the driveway of an estate with a French Normandy Tutor style arch. "It's right here," he said.

I squinted my eyes, doing a double take. "Is that a giant pineapple in your driveway?"

He chuckled. "It does look like a pineapple, now that you say that."

"It's not a pineapple?" My eyes were glued to the ginormous sculpture while we walked closer. "What's it supposed to be?"

"It's like a couple of vases stacked with some trees planted in them." He pointed to the center. "Can you see it better now?"

"I've never seen such an elaborate driveway ornament."

"That might be another thing not to talk about." Wally's voice was careful. "My mom loves it, but my dad still has a sore spot."

"Why?" I felt myself relax as I enjoyed learning another piece of random history from Wally's childhood.

"So, the short story is my mom fell in love with it when we were vacationing in the Cayman Islands. So, she bought it."

My grin stretched tight across my face in anticipation. "And, why is your dad sore?"

"You see how big it is?"

"Yeah."

"The Cayman Islands are tiny islands in the Caribbean thousands of miles from here. A normal souvenir would be some shampoo or a rock that fits in your pocket."

"So, he's mad because of having to send it here."

"You don't just send a giant pineapple in the mail. We had to hire a moving company, but it got super weird because of the international thing." He pointed to the sculpture with comedic hostility. "I could write a book about that experience. Let's not talk about it."

I tried to stifle my laugh, but I couldn't hold it back.

"You better shut that off before we go inside." He pointed to my lips, now tightly holding a giggle. "Or my dad's going find out why you're laughing, and this day is going to be ruined!"

He was teasing, and it made me give up, and I let my laugh out again. "It's just too funny." I tried to compose myself while Wally opened the door and led the way inside. Here we go, I thought to myself.

Chapter Twenty

We were greeted by the tall, wooden staircase that framed the outside living room wall. My shoulders relaxed when the aroma of sage and rosemary wafted up my nose like it was sent to awaken the holiday cheer inside me. An elderly woman sat in an armchair facing us. "Is that Wally?" she asked.

"Yes, Nana, and I brought a friend too."

"You did?" Her eyes never flickered, nor did her head move to greet me. "Who?"

"Her name is Aubergine," he called to her in a loud, measured voice, but then whispered under his breath to me, "Nana's a hundred and two, and she can't hear or see well."

"Bring her here so I can see her." Her voice was deep for a woman but spry, matching her facial expression.

Wally gave me a nod that told me to walk first. I took a couple steps, then looked back to make sure he was following me. I walked right up to Nana and opened my hand into a soft wave as I approached her. "Hi."

"Hello." She pointed to the patterned sofa across from her chair. "You sit and make yourself at home."

Smoothing the back of my skirt under me when I sat, I made sure to remember my lady manners. Something about the way she sat with perfect posture made me know that she was a woman with old-fashioned etiquette. I rested the flowers across my lap, securing them with one hand.

Her blue-gray eyes fixed on me. "Are you a friend from school?"

"No, we met through a mutual friend."

"Relax," she insisted. "You look like you're at the dentist." Her dimpled chin cracked deeper from her smile.

"Sorry." The old Abs would have made a sarcastic comment to ward off any awkwardness but socializing with manners was still new to me.

"Abs doesn't go to school," Wally said. "She works in fashion." I gave him a small smile as I was thankful that he was helping me navigate the small talk, and I picked up on his conversation starter.

"I actually do school online."

Wally nodded in recognition. "Oh yeah, I keep forgetting about that."

"And what sort of work do you do in fashion?" Nana asked.

"Not much fashion. More assisting. I work for a woman's clothing designer, so I do mostly packing and shipping. We're getting ready to open a store on Monday. It's a lot of retail stuff."

"You like clothes?"

My heart melted a little when the conversation turned to something I loved. I answered her confidently, "I love clothes. It's pretty much the only thing I'm good at."

"Ah, you're young. You'll have lots of stuff you'll be good at yet."

"I don't know," I said with a doubtful pitch in my voice. "The more I'm around it, the more I love it. And actually—" I felt myself shift toward her to engage better "—I saw your photo at the theatre, the one with that beaded dress. I love that dress. I can't stop thinking about it."

Her head tilted thoughtfully to the side. "I remember the dress you're talking about. It had pearl strands sewn over a white slip dress."

"Yeah, that sounds like the one. It was stunning on you. I love that style. It pops your face right out of the picture." I glanced at Wally to make sure I was still minding my manners, and he wasn't giving me a warning glare for talking about the wrong stuff. His face confirmed he was happy and maybe even enjoying the conversation.

"I haven't thought about that dress in years. That was my aunt's dress. She had bought it in the early twenties, but she saved it for me. I think I was maybe fifteen when I wore it."

"You were just a baby," I said.

"We grew up a lot faster those days than kids now. I was married when I was eighteen."

"I didn't realize you were that young," Wally said, an air of awe in his voice. "How old was Grandpa?"

"He was nineteen. We were young, but that's how we did it back then." She shrugged and looked to Wally. "You know, dinner won't be done for an hour or so . . . why don't you run up and grab the dress? I'd like to take a look at it."

My body froze, and my eyes widen. "You still have it?" I leaned forward. "In this house?"

"I'm sure it's in a trunk in the attic. I kept most of my costume dresses. Wally's mother used to play dress up in them when she was little, and I saved them in case one day I'd have a granddaughter. Well, that never happened, but it must be up there. I know I never got rid of it."

I looked at Wally to plead with my eyes to get the dress. I'm sure the look on my face resembled a dog waiting for his favorite treat. Wally gave in and stood up. "Come on, we can go dig it out." His voice was amused. "But first, let's go say hi to my parents."

We walked through the open French doors that led into the dining room, already set for our meal with white dinnerware and amber-colored cloth napkins. The kitchen was through a door in the back of the dining room. His mom was leaning over the open oven, freshening the glaze on the turkey, and his dad lowered the book he was reading on the kitchen table when he saw us walk in. "Wally and Aubergine are here," he said to his wife.

"Hi, honey." She glanced at Wally but kept her hands steady over the turkey and continued to pour a glaze over it. Then her eyes stopped on me. "We're glad you came to see us. Do you need something to drink?"

"I'm fine for now but thank you. I brought you some flowers." I extended my hand with the bouquet.

"Those are lovely. Thank you." She looked back to Wally and asked, "Could you please grab a vase down from the cabinet?"

Wally reached into the small cabinet above the fridge and pulled out a white vase, filled it with water from the sink and handed it to me. I took the vase and set it on the counter. Then slipping the plastic sleeve off the flowers, I arranged them in the vase. "How does that look?" I asked Wally's mom.

"It's lovely. I'll take them and put them on the table." I handed her the vase, and she walked back into the dining room with them.

Wally called after her, "We're going to go get a dress for Nana from the attic."

"That's fine," his mom said.

Wally opened a skinny door in the back of the kitchen. "This leads upstairs." He waited for me to follow him.

"I feel sort of dumb, but I don't know your mom's name," I said once we got to the top of the stairs.

"It's Claire."

My mouth fell open. "You're kidding. That's my mom's name."

"Really? That's pretty cool."

"At least I won't have a hard time remembering it." My mind instantly flashed to an image of my mom with her fuzzy unibrow. Making the comparison between the two women, I noted that Wally got the better Claire. It was okay though. I wasn't going to dwell on it today. Although I did find it humorous this was the first time I had thought of my mom on Thanksgiving, and it took me less than a second to push her image out of my mind. I was enjoying my dress hunt, and I wanted to keep my spirits up.

Wally opened a small door at the end of the upstairs hall, revealing another staircase. "You might have to duck your head a little when you go up these," he warned when he went first into the attic. The room was unusually well lit for a storage area, as it had windows on all four walls. Wally walked past the stacks of boxes in front to select a German-style trunk along the back wall.

"It has to be in here. I used to play hide-and-seek up here all the time, and I remember seeing it." He flipped the lid open. Nothing was organized or sealed for preservation, and it looked like kids had been playing in it. He dug right to the bottom of the trunk and pulled it out like it was a worthless rag. "It's heavy."

I reached out to receive it with both hands like I was rescuing it. "I can't believe it was shoved in there."

"I think it had been packed away neatly at one time, but a few years ago, my little cousins were up here digging around."

"Shame on them." I spread it out, letting the skirt drape over my lap. The seams were still tight, but many of the beads drooped loosely on their strings. Even more strings hung bare and broken. "These were all hand sewn. It's a crazy amount of work," I said. "It would take weeks to make one dress."

"That's probably why they didn't stay in style very long."

I hugged the dress to my chest, feeling sad for the shape it was now in. "It belongs in a museum, not crumbled up in a trunk."

Wally grinned at me like he was getting a kick out of my despair over a dress. "I don't think anyone else falls in love with clothes the way you do."

"Do you think I'm weird?" I asked more to make fun of myself than to get a serious answer.

His eyes were gentle when they rested on mine. "Nah, I don't think you're weird at all."

Chapter Twenty-One

"I brought the whole trunk down," Wally announced when he clumsily lugged Nana's trunk, clunking it on every step, down into the family room and dropped it near Nana's feet. "You have a few dresses in there, and Abs wanted to ask you about them."

I held up the beaded dress I had lovingly carried in my arms all the way downstairs. "This is the one from the picture."

Nana gently took it from me. "I remember it was the most uncomfortable dress I ever had because you can't relax in it. You sit on a bunch of beads. No matter what type of surface you sit on, you always notice it."

"I never thought about that. What a bummer," I replied. "Now that you say that, I can see how it would be a pain in the butt."

"Literally." She sweetly chuckled at my pun. "I put it on to sing and then took it off as soon as I was off stage." She held it up, reaching it out to me to put away. Craning her neck to see into the trunk, she asked, "What else is in there?"

I replaced the beaded dress in the trunk, and I pulled out a midnight blue dress with a cinched waist and a long flowing

A-lined skirt. "This is my new favorite when I saw it," I talked while I walked it over to her. "It's like a Cinderella dress."

"Ah, that's a Dior." She reached her arms forward again, taking the dress from me, resting it on her lap. "Those dresses came after the beaded ones. Dior's dresses were classy and elegant."

"I adore it."

"You can see the difference in their styles. Dior made his dresses to make you feel like a woman." She pointed near the tiny waist. "Look how it brings in the waist."

"I can't believe you wore these dresses. They seem so formal compared to what everyone wears now."

"The way people dressed was always formal back then. It was a sign of respect to dress appropriately when you were seen in public. Women always wore dresses and long coats and gloves. I never left the house without my hair done. People behaved better because of it."

"How do you mean?" I asked, sitting again on the sofa right next to her. I was so intrigued by Nana, I could have sat all night and talked about clothes.

"Well, look at people today; they have no respect. It is my belief you behave differently when you are dressed appropriately, and people treat you with respect when you are dressed to receive it."

I stole a look at Wally, thinking he would be bored with all the fashion gossip, but he appeared to be content to sit with us. "What was your favorite dress?" I asked.

"That's hard to say. You can't compare them because as the style changed, so did my preferences. Times change. So does fashion."

I thought about how fashion had evolved so much and said, "I used to love the clothes I wore, but after you look back and see where it came from, I can't even compare what I am wearing to these gowns. I think everything in style today is ugly now."

Nana flipped the Dior dress over, continuing to examine it, picking tiny lint balls off as she found them. "A lot of it is. But you don't notice it because everyone's wearing it."

Wally's mom quietly appeared in the doorway, still holding her oven mitt. "I hope everyone's hungry," she said, "because it's ready." She smiled warmly at me when I got up to follow Wally, and added, "I'm so happy you made time to come see us."

Her direct attention did a lot to help put me at ease, and I immediately replied, "It's my pleasure. I'm really glad I came too."

Dinner was quiet but not uncomfortable. Sitting next to Wally, across from his parents with Nana at the head chair, I heeded Wally's warning about avoiding certain conversations. I mostly smiled and complimented the food. Henry sporadically quizzed Wally about his classes and his other friends. I could tell Wally was getting annoyed, so as soon as I finished my plate, I excused myself to use the restroom, thinking Wally might need a break from me overhearing all the details of his life.

Taking an extra moment to groom, I smoothed out my hair. I had been trying to control my thoughts, but here I was wondering how Fulton was doing at Candace's parents' house. Her folks would love him. I tried to avoid the feelings but found myself wishing Fulton was here instead of Wally. I scolded myself and returned my mind back to the present, reminding myself to be grateful for Wally's and his family's hospitality.

When I walked back down the staircase, I didn't mean to eavesdrop, but Nana spoke in such a loud voice it was hard to not hear. I slowed, not wanting to intrude on something I wasn't supposed to hear. "Well, I like her better than Denise," I heard Nana proclaim like everyone was hard of hearing.

I crouched on the stairs when I realized she was talking about me. "You're not talking to her anymore, are you?" Henry asked in a tone that sounded more of an interrogation than an inquiry.

Wally spoke quietly and I had a hard time hearing his answer, so I crept forward, but I still didn't make out what he said.

"Let's not talk about her," Henry said. "It's rude. We're happy to have Aubergine here. Glad you're making better judgments."

"She's not my girlfriend. She's a friend whose family is out of state. She didn't have plans and was going to spend the day alone, so I offered for her to come here. I'm not hiding anything from you about her."

"She has a fellow?" Henry asked.

"Not that I know of, but that's *not* my business." Wally sounded annoyed.

"Then you know what they say," Henry said.

"Mind your own business," Wally said.

"Poop or get off the pot," Nana chimed in her loud voice.

There was silence from the room, as nobody received Nana's comment as a joke, but I struggled to hold back a giggle. It was too funny to hear Nana give out dating advice and talk about pooh at the same time. Feeling ashamed for listening, I knew I had been gone too long already, so I stood up and cleared my throat loudly to announce I was coming down the stairs. Then I walked back into the dining room. "Sorry it took me so long." I smiled at Wally, who looked relieved I was back in the room.

Claire stood up. "Would anyone like pie?"

I was full but wanted to make the best impression, so I remained standing and said, "I would love some, and may I help you in the kitchen?"

"Sure. I would like that." She went through the door, and I followed. "You can grab some plates down from there." She pointed to a cabinet next to the sink.

I reached into the cupboard and took out five small round plates, setting them next to the pie on the kitchen counter. "That looks yummy." I inhaled the smell of nutmeg.

"Thanks. I like to bake when someone other than myself is around to eat it." She sliced the pie with eight big cuts through the center. I held one plate out at a time for her to place a slice onto. Then we carried the pie plates back to the dining room, rejoining everyone at the table.

Having only taken one bite, I was savoring the sting of the nutmeg when Nana loudly picked up the conversation and asked me, "Do you play poker?"

Glancing over to Wally, I checked if gambling was an appropriate topic. Since Nana brought it up, and he didn't give me any indication to avoid it, I answered, "Not a whole lot. I think I might have tried it once or twice. How about you?"

"I like to play."

"She cheats," Wally said through a mouthful of pie.

Her eyes narrowed playfully as she retorted back, "I do not."

"Okay, not cheating. We'll call it selective seeing when it comes to her card playing," Wally clarified.

I enjoyed the playful banter Wally had with Nana. Their bond was evident through the little faces they gave each other. "You're going to have to see for yourself," Nana leaned over the table, insistently. "Would you like to play?"

"I can, but I don't remember how. I might need to have a practice round."

"It's easy," Wally said. "You can play a hand with me first until you get the hang of it."

I finished my pie and set my fork on my plate. "Sure, that sounds fun," I said. Then I stood and picked up mine and Wally's empty plate. "Let me help clean up first."

"No, you're our guest, dear." Claire immediately stood up and took the plates from my hand. "Go ahead and get settled into the family room."

Wally gave me the nod to head over. I hesitated to agree because I had a hunch, I was about to get my butt kicked, but I was oddly looking forward to it. I flashed an genuine smile at Nana and said, "Go easy on me."

"Oh, there'll be no going easy on anyone," she declared, and then dramatically lowered her voice into a conniving sounding cackle that seemed too funny to come out of someone as little and fragile looking as her. Everyone in the room burst out laughing.

We played poker way past dark, and the night air had turned crisp, and snowflakes started to dot the sidewalk, warning of a blizzard. I rushed to catch the last train back to the city. "I can't believe I stayed so late. I hope I didn't overstay my welcome," I said to Wally, who insisted on walking me to the station.

"I would have let you know if you needed to leave." Wally's smile was approving. "I'm glad you came. Nana enjoyed talking to you."

"She's so cute. Has she always lived with you?" I asked.

"As long as I can remember."

"I can tell you have a great relationship."

"She's always been easy for me to talk to. I think when you get that old, you've been through a lot, and you learn things have a way of working out. My mom always worries about everything so much. It has been hard to be truly honest with her because she gets so dramatic."

"So, you don't tell her what you're really up to?" I teased. A snowflake landed in my eyelash, and I blinked it away.

"Not even close."

I smoothed a lock of hair out of my face, wondering if I should confess what I had overheard. Part of me knew to mind my own business, but Wally wasn't the type to get mad, and I was curious. "So . . ." I started in a prying tone then paused, waiting for him to respond.

"So . . ." he echoed. "What do you want to know?"

"I should maybe keep my mouth shut, but I feel sort of guilty."

"Why?"

"I overheard your parents asking you about me when I was in the bathroom."

He nodded in recognition. "Then you know how they are."

"They were asking you about a different girl."

"Denise."

"Is that an old girlfriend?"

"Not really an *old* girlfriend. More like an off-and-on girlfriend."

"I've never seen you with her. You must be off now?"

He brushed the budding snowflakes off his coat, one sleeve at a time, then finally said, "It's hard to explain."

"You can try."

"I never even told them about her, but they found out. She's older than I am. They hate that. They don't even want to give her a chance." He rolled his eyes. "They're so traditional."

"But you like her?" I watched the side of his face, waiting for his eyes to confirm what he wouldn't tell me.

"I've been avoiding her lately. I know that's messed up, but when we're together we get along great, but I've noticed if I don't see her, I don't think about her. I'm starting to think that's the bigger indicator of how I feel. Like, shouldn't the person you're meant to be with matter when you're not with them?" he pondered out loud.

His words reminded me of how I spent the day with him, having a wonderful time, but my mind kept pulling my thoughts to Fulton. Wally must have read my mind when I didn't say anything, because he added, "Don't you think about Fulton when he's not around?"

I bit my lip, not wanting to hurt his feelings, so I came up with, "Fulton's not my boyfriend."

"I don't know why he isn't." His words came out with a hint of hopelessness that made me giggle. "Why are you laughing?" he asked, now starting to echo my laughter.

"I think it's one of those things that if I didn't laugh about it, I'd probably cry."

His already smooth dark eyes softened even more when he held my gaze. "That bad?"

I turned my face down, observing our feet step forward, now making prints in the accumulated snow. "I don't know if it's . . ." I started to say bad, but it didn't feel bad. I felt good until I started thinking about Candace, and then I felt bad, but Fulton didn't make me feel bad. I was confused. "I don't know," I repeated, still not knowing how to finish the sentence, so I repeated it again, this time with closure. "I just don't know."

"Well, glad we solved that crisis."

The way Wally smiled at me made me laugh. "Sorry, I don't mean to be a bummer." I tried to smooth away the serious tone to the conversation and change the subject. "So, your parents think I'm your girlfriend?"

"My parents are annoying," he picked up the conversation. "Like, okay, here's how they are. They don't like Denise, so I don't bring her around. Problem solved, right?"

"Right." I wasn't sure where he was going with this example, but I agreed.

"Then they saw me working concessions with you that night at the theatre, and without even asking, they assume you are my new girlfriend."

"Wasn't your dad just teasing?"

"No, right after that he offered me the Saturday comedy slot. I knew it was some sort of bribery to stay away from Denise."

I gave him my best skeptical look, still not convinced his parents would be that calculated. "I'm the reason you got a promotion?"

"It's not really a promotion. It's more of a blackmail."

"Then why did you take it?"

"Who wouldn't headline their own show when given the chance? It's not going to affect the way I feel about a girl. In fact, at first it only made me want to see Denise more."

"But you don't feel like that anymore?"

"I think she's great." He shoved his hands into his side coat pockets, looking straight ahead. He said in a voice that seemed to be distant, "But I don't know if it's normal to not think about her when she's not around."

"Did you think about her today?"

"Yeah, because everyone keeps asking me about her."

"Aside from that?"

"Honestly? No, I was content the way things were." He looked at me briefly before turning his focus back to walking, but not before I saw how sweet his brown eyes were. Then he added, "I had a great day."

"I had a good day too." I twisted the ends of my lips up to give him a reassuring smile. I did have a perfect day, but I still thought about Fulton most of the day. *That must have meant something.*

Chapter Twenty-Two

When I dragged my algebra-hung-overed-body back to the store
Monday morning, I was met with half a dozen new hires who
had started training. Their excitement rubbed off on me—a little.
However, Gabby was on edge, and her mood was outweighing any
of their positive effect on me.

"We moved the desks to the back room now," Gabby explained
when I walked in. "You're going to be squeezed in the corner way
in the back."

"That's fine." I dodged the filled clothing racks scattered in our
new floor set and made my way back. "What do you need me to do
today?" I called back to her when she followed me.

"I'm letting the store staff handle all the freight and
merchandising now," she thought out loud. "If you want to go
over the graphics your dad sent and do a last look at the email
templates and promos that are going to be sent out, I'd love an extra
set of eyes on those."

"Sure." I pursed my lips forward, while I did a mental inventory of how much work that was going to be. "Do you have a file for them?"

"Yeah, the graphics are all in a tall box in the back, and I already forwarded you the templates."

My good mood soared as I realized I was off freight duty. "Anything else?"

"Can you price some hors d'oeuvres from a couple different places to get an idea of what we can serve for our private night?"

I plopped on my desk chair and booted up my computer. "I can do that."

"Good. Email me what you find out. I need to leave now for meetings." Her voice trailed off as she checked her phone for messages. I waited for her to get done reading, then her eyes floated back up, but she still looked distracted. "Okay, I'm out of here for the rest of the day. Lexi's here too, so if she needs help, try to assist her."

"Sure." I waited for her to leave and then I opened my email on my computer and scrolled down until I found the one from Gabby with the templates. I found ads dated for the private night and one for the grand opening, but nothing for holiday promotion, which I thought was odd. Rather than call Gabby, who I knew was busy, I dialed my dad.

"Morning, Abs," he greeted me.

"Morning."

"How are you?"

"I'm fine. I'm at work. Gabby wanted me to look through the templates you made for her. I'm wondering if you made anything for regular holiday promotion?"

"I'm getting those out today. Sorry. I took a couple days off for Thanksgiving."

"Okay. I was just checking."

"Did you end up going with your friend for Thanksgiving?"

"I did. Sorry, that's why I didn't call. I didn't get home until late. Then I worked on my homework the rest of the weekend."

"That's fine. I figured you were busy. How did it go?"

"It went awesome. I ended up talking to his Nana most of the time about fashion. She has all these vintage gowns she let me look at." Then sighing like I was being tossed into a princess dream land, I closed my eyes to linger on the memory and added, "I loved it."

"What dresses are you talking about," he inquired further. "How old?"

"She had a trunk full of every style. I loved the ones from the nineteen-thirties with the long flowy skirts." I found myself fanning my hands over my own jeans to illustrate a flowing dress even though no one was in the room to see it. "It made me think today's fashion is so boring. I mean, really, I have jeans and a duster sweater on right now."

"You don't like clothes now?" he teased.

"I didn't say that," I lightly snapped back, then hugged my free arm over my chest. "I just don't understand how it changed so much. How does it go from getting to wear these elegant day dresses every day to looking like you're going to go shovel some hay?"

My dad's amused chuckle piped through the phone. "Our society has changed a lot, if you haven't noticed, but I think most of the drastic transformation was brought about with the industrial revolution. Then after that, it's the designers who set the trends. People buy what is in fashion."

Leaning way back on my chair, I lifted my feet up to rest on the top of my desk. This topic was so captivating, I settled in, getting comfortable to chat longer, "It was so fascinating to talk to her about it."

"History is interesting. It doesn't surprise me that the first time you realize you like history, it's the history of fashion."

"It was sort of cool being with Wally's family because his parents are older too and very traditional. They have this older home, and I felt like I went back in time."

"I'm glad you had fun," he said, then added, "I was thinking about you."

I didn't want to confess that I purposely didn't think about them. Instead, I asked, "Did you guys have a nice day?"

"We did. We shared dinner with the Rogers." My dad spoke fast, hinting he didn't want to talk about their weekend, and he confirmed my hunch by changing the subject back to me. "The big store opens next week, right?"

"Yeah, I'm excited. We have all this extra help now too, so I should be able to pass some of my duties off to them. It's going to be a crazy December."

"Are you still planning on coming home for a few days for Christmas?"

"I am . . ." My oral confirmation felt more like a reminder, telling myself to start emotionally preparing to see my mom for the first time since I had moved back to the city. A hollowing that always started in my gut—when I thought about my mom—echoed, rising into my chest, but thankfully my dad didn't bring her up.

"We are looking forward to it. Eddie said Fulton's coming home next week already when he gets done with class. He'll be here a couple weeks, but you probably know that since you see him all the time."

"Not that much anymore . . ." My voice trailed off to avoid giving him any hints about how I was really feeling about Fulton. "But I suppose I'm at work." I sat forward again, returning my feet back to the floor. "I'd better get going here."

"Alright, talk to you soon. Bye."

"Yep. Bye." I ended my call as a new girl walked into the backroom. "Hi," I greeted her. "Can I help you with something?"

"I'm looking for the bathroom."

"Right in that door." I pointed to the darkened room in the corner. "But, just an FYI, there's a trick to the toilet; you have to flush it and then quick flush it again or it doesn't get enough power."

"Good to know." She smirked like she was trying to hold back a giggle, and then she disappeared inside the bathroom.

I closed out of my email and opened a search window to look for restaurants nearby that delivered. The first place to pop up was the restaurant Fulton had offered to take me to for my birthday. Maybe my computer was trying to remind me of a reason to not like him. But it didn't work. *Now, I was thinking about him again!* I took a long breath and scrolled down, making the Greek restaurant disappear off the top of my page, wishing it was that easy to scroll through my own thoughts.

Chapter Twenty-Three

Before I knew it, our store's private night arrived. Everyone buzzed around with an extra sense of urgency while they waited to welcome their friends and family. We had each been allowed to invite up to twenty people to shop and use our discounts to provide the sales staff with an opportunity to practice their service skills before opening to the public.

Lexi had decorated the store to look like a Christmas village with miniature artificial trees and fake snow in the window. I personally didn't think Christmas tree village went well with high fashion, but Lexi insisted it helped get customers in the buying spirit.

So, as I balanced on one leg on top of a ladder, trying to hang the last of my window graphics, Gabby came out of the backroom and declared, "Alright, everyone. I'm unlocking the door. It's time." Her eyes—echoing of a forced confidence—met mine. "Would you like to greet everyone and collect their invitation cards?"

"Sure," I eagerly agreed. I did one final tug on the left hook to make sure it would hold my sign and then descended the ladder.

Gabby handed me a wide wicker basket. "Make sure anyone who comes in has a card. I don't want people sneaking in that aren't supposed to be here. Any press before we are ready could be bad."

I hooked my arm through the arched handle of the basket, put on my best happy smile, and said, "Deal." Then hearing a scuffle at the door, Gabby and I both turned our heads to see two middle-aged women coming in. Gabby winked at me and walked away.

Little butterflies in my stomach boosted my energy level when I greeted the ladies and took their cards. *We were officially opened!* I tried to avoid staring at them, so I forced myself to watch out the door, but it didn't take long before another person came and then another. We had a slow trickle of customers the whole night, keeping me busy. When I finally had time to survey the store, it was packed with at least a couple dozen shoppers who appeared to be enjoying themselves. Then I noticed one of the new girls coming out of the backroom, her eyes shifting around the room like she was looking for something. "Do you need something?" I called over to her.

"Can you come here?" She concealed a wave toward her.

I did a fast survey out the door, down each side of the sidewalk, and saw that no one was coming, then I left my basket with the cashier and walked back. "What's going on?" I asked when I approached.

Her cheeks were noticeably flushed, and even more surprising the tips of her ponytail looked damp. Before I had time to ask if she had been ill, she cracked the backroom door open, and a slow-moving pool of water met my feet. My eyes widened in a frenzy as they followed the source coming from under the closed bathroom door. Her face reddened even more. "The toilet's going crazy," she whispered.

"You have to shut the water off!" I screamed in a panic. With a hard cringe on my face, I sacrificed my new pair of heels and plowed through the puddle. I yanked on the bathroom door, allowing another rush of water to equalize into the backroom. Sucking in my breath so hard it made a squeaking noise, I could only whimper now at the thought of my shoes, swimming in pooh water. With no time to grieve, I lunged forward toward a spiral gush rocketing water out of the toilet bowel like Old Faithful. I reached down below the toilet right into the geyser. Water completely drenched me, but somehow, I was able to turn the water main off. My breath slowed just as the water slowed. When it finally stopped, I let out a long-defeated sigh.

I resisted looking down at my shoes as I knew they were a total fashion casualty at this point. Even worse, the water made a disgusting squishing sound as I walked. "You gotta get the mop bucket," I instructed the salesgirl but then halted fast on my heels when I saw a woman standing outside the bathroom recording me with her smartphone. "Put that away." I held my hand up to stop her. Then I scolded her again. "No filming!" I waved my hand in front of the camera, but it was too late. The social media world already saw it under the headline, "Gabby Rue's New Store is a Total Disaster."

Gabby tried to hide her disappointment, but I could see it in the tightness of her lips when she let me go home since I was soaked and totally embarrassed. I had convinced myself that nobody would care, but then I got a text from Tina, who I hadn't talked to in months.

Tina: *You alright?*
Me: *Yeah. Why?*
Tina: *I thought you'd be sick or something. I saw you clogged the toilet. What, you take a giant duber? LOL!!!!!*

I threw my face into my hands, stifling a high-pitched scream. *People thought I clogged the toilet!* I was about to lose my mind from humiliation when it hit me. A year ago, I didn't even have social media. People honestly don't know how to live without it anymore. That woman whipped out her phone and started filming when she had no clue who I was. She had no regard for my privacy. I never thought I would admit it, but social media had a way of sucking. I never had to worry about that happening in Montana. Okay, I just freaked myself out a little. I wasn't supposed to have positive thoughts about Montana.

I couldn't reply to Tina. She wasn't trying to be a friend. All she wanted was a laugh. I was about to stuff my phone back into my pocket when it beeped again. *Don't read it,* I agonized to myself. As painful as I knew it would be, I lowered my eyes and read:

Dad: *You okay?*

Me: *Yeah. I didn't break the toilet! I was helping a girl. I don't want to talk about it. Going home to get dry clothes.*

Dad: *Okay.*

Another text came through.

Wally: *You doing okay?*

Me: *Yes. Don't want to talk about it.*

Wally: *Okay.*

My fingers were trembling when I held in the off button on my phone. Desperate for some distance, I vowed to keep my phone off and work on my algebra the rest of the night—anything was better than having to field these texts.

Chapter Twenty-Four

I laid low after my embarrassing episode and was actually sort of excited to get out of the city when it was time to go to my parents' place. With my plane landing in Montana after midnight, I struggled to keep my eyes open. The dark Montana sky wore a shade of gray that could only be described as cold gray. I ducked my head into my coat collar to avoid the wind while I ran to my dad's pickup. Luckily it was still warmish, and my dad was right behind me to start it up and get on our way home. "There's a storm moving in, so we'd better get home fast." He stretched his neck to see over the bottom layer of fog on the windshield.

Dad sped down the interstate, passing no cars. With the stars tucked away for the night, the only light was from our headlights and the reflection they made off the falling snow. The snow thickened into a blizzard. With visibility nonexistent, my dad relied on his memory to where the road had been. "I don't think we should be out here," I said. I tried to help my dad navigate the road, but the combination of my heavy eyes and the repetitive motion of watching the snow fly in front of the window had a hypnotizing effect on me, making me drowsier.

"I'm not pulling over because we'll get buried. We're supposed to get over eighteen inches this weekend," he said.

I raised my eyebrows, wondering why I bothered to come back home. I had forgotten how miserable Montana winters could be. Now I worried I would get snowed in and not be able to leave. Somehow, we made it to the farm. Dad parked the truck, and I trudged through the snow but stopped before I made it to the porch. The tiny home was welcoming me with a glowing light on the porch and another one in the window, but all I had was a feeling of dread. "Please, don't let this be bad," I prayed and followed my dad inside.

My dad slipped off his lace-up boots, setting them near the wood stove to dry. In a hushed voice he said, "Mom's sleeping, so be quiet."

I nodded, relieved I would have no drama tonight.

"You hungry?" he whispered.

I gave my head a silent side-to-side shake. "I'm okay," I insisted. Then I pointed to the back of the house and added in a hushed voice, "I need to use the bathroom, but I'll be quiet."

"Alright, then I'll see you in the morning, honey." Dad leaned in for a hug, and I squeezed him back. Then I tiptoed through my nighttime routine and headed up to my loft. Remembering it being tiny, I was taken aback by how small everything in the house was. It certainly didn't give me any feelings of nostalgia. I didn't miss this place at all.

I scooted onto the center of my bed and crawled under the blankets. My bones were still chilled, and I shivered as I wiggled deeper into the warmth of the bed. I couldn't close my eyes until I stole a peek out of my window. It was a habit that, even now that I didn't live here, I couldn't break. The storm had picked up more, and I couldn't see the mountain or the Rogers' house. It was a total whiteout. I let out a nervous sigh, hoping I wouldn't get stuck here. *That would be bad.*

I slept in late despite the fact I could hear someone in the kitchen. I had forgotten how noisy it was to live with other people. When I could no longer put off my stomach pains, I mustered up the most positive attitude I could and went downstairs. My dad was reading on the couch, and my mom was adding ingredients to a pot simmering on the stove.

"Morning," I said in a sleepy voice on my way to the bathroom.

"Morning," Dad said.

"Welcome home," my mom said as she turned from her project. I felt like a cat trying to escape a new person by scurrying around the side parameters of the room. "How were your flights?" Mom asked.

"Fine." I ducked into the bathroom and shut the door behind me. Then I scolded myself for acting so uptight. *Get a grip,* I told myself. She is your mom. You can act normal. But as I freshened up, I thought about how little I had talked to my mom these last few months. It was impossible to gauge what kind of mood she would be in over the phone so I had avoided her as much as I could. Now that I was here, avoidance wasn't an option. Almost on cue, my stomach reminded me again to find some food, so I was forced to join them.

"Coffee?" my mom offered when she saw me come out of the bathroom.

"Sure." I hesitantly lowered myself onto a chair in the corner; my eyes found a pan of homemade cinnamon rolls in the middle of the table. I pointed to the pan. "May I help myself?"

My mom placed my coffee cup next to me. "Go ahead."

"Thanks." I lifted a fluffy corner roll out of the pan, dropping it onto a plate that my mom had handed me. "What's new here?" I asked, then leaned over my plate and took a bite of roll from my fork. I didn't really want to hear about the farm news, but I had vowed to try my best to be pleasant.

Mom gave my dad one of her looks that said she had news. I was taken back since I hadn't seen this look in a while, and it usually proceeded a terrible idea that would negatively alter my life forever. "Should we tell her?" Mom asked.

My dad put his book down and came over to sit next to me. "If you want." To my horror he also had that look in his eyes like he had a secret.

"Sure," she said. I watched her pour another cup of coffee. I studied her hands, her arms, her face, her back. Something had to be wrong with her, but I didn't see it. She took the cup and handed it to my dad.

"Thanks, dear," my dad said. He smiled lovingly at my mom and took his cup, setting it next to mine on the table. He adjusted himself to get comfortable. *A talk was coming.* I had just swallowed another bite of my roll. I felt my stomach asking for more, but my brain was telling me to stay alert and not get distracted. Whatever was coming was big.

"Tell me what?" I dared to look at my mom. This had to be her deal, whatever it was. It was *always* her deal.

"We need to have a talk about your internship and school, so let's start there," Dad said.

"Okay . . .What about it?" I searched his face for clues.

"After Christmas is usually when seniors start to get serious about their plans for the following year. College applications are due in a couple months. Have you thought about what you're going to do after school?"

"Not really." I looked at him suspiciously because I knew something else was up. This was just the breaking-the-ice question. Then I added, "I've been busy."

"Do you want to go to college?" he asked.

My eyebrows furloughed. This was like being asked to guess how many gumballs were in a bathtub-sized jar. "I don't know."

"Have you looked at your options?" My dad's gaze was steady on me and in an uncomfortable way, he was forcing me to look back at him. He continued, "They have lots of great fashion programs right in the city. You could study merchandising, or design, or management."

"I don't want to do management," I thought out loud. "Why can't I continue what I'm doing?"

"We talked about this." His eyebrows lifted. "Remember?"

"All you said was it was unpaid, and I'd have to get a paid job. What if I get a job being an assistant that pays?"

"That's an option," he agreed. "However, I would think most designers are going to want you to have more skills than you have, and you might need to go to college to get more training. A lot of assistants manage social media and marketing. I don't mind helping with that now, but if this is your career choice then you're going to need those skills yourself. You would need to start taking a few classes to help build your resume."

I rubbed my temples, not wanting to think about more school. Work was enough without school. "I haven't really thought about all this," I admitted again.

"I know you haven't, but you need to start. Before you go back to New York in two days, I want you to have two different possible plans laid out. You only have a few short months before you'll need to start paying your own rent, and homelessness is not an option I'm okay with for you. You need a plan. Okay?" His brown eyes were caring but insistent.

"I understand." I picked at my roll, thinking I should have eaten it right away when I had an appetite. Now I was depressed.

"Don't waste your youth stumbling around," he warned. "So many people reach forty and realize they wasted half their life. It's time to pick a star to wish on."

"How do you know which one to pick?" I asked but wasn't really wanting him to answer. I felt like being difficult because my dad's marketing pitches always annoyed me. I wasn't picking a star. That would have been easy. You look and see they are all the same. Then you point at one. Wow, that's not hard at all. I needed a life. This was harder.

"There was a study published a few years ago that looked at what people regret the most in life," my dad started to explain. "And it turned out people didn't regret doing anything they did that didn't work out, or anything they did badly. The thing they regretted the most was not taking the chances. So, I'm not sure it matters if you pick the right one right away because your path might not even be fully visible right now. You start with the stars that you can see now and just go for it. As you move closer to it, you may like what you see and want to keep going in that direction, or you may decide a different one looks brighter. As long as you are moving toward one in particular, you are moving forward. Life goes fast, and if you're not moving forward, the world will push you back. Don't take my word for it. Ask anyone who is over forty. Life is fleeting. Don't waste life stumbling. You'll regret it." He reached forward, and placed his hand on mine, and gave it a fatherly squeeze. "You need a goal."

My dad always knew how to drive a point home with the right words to connect to each person. Stumbling was a four-letter word to my former dancing self. I'd rather have my oxygen cut off than stumble on stage. But I didn't feel like I was ready to decide on a path. As if he felt my need for a conversation change, he said, "There's another thing we need to talk about that could change your plans for next year." My dad adjusted himself again, this time leaning back like he was welcoming my mom into the conversation. "Your mom and I are moving."

"What do you mean?" I sat up straighter. This was the last thing I had expected to hear.

My mom picked up the dialogue. "I've always wanted to live closer to my sister in Vermont, so I decided now was the time."

I let out a snort so loud, I could swear Fulton heard it across the yard. *That was a load of baloney because my mom hated her sister!* My eyes darted to my dad for him to give me the real reason they were moving to Vermont, but his face was unreadable. "You're going to live next to Kim?" I questioned, waiting for the punchline.

"I think it would be good for us to be closer to family," my mom continued. "These last few months of being out here with no one but the Rogers' has been sort of lonesome for me. I think I'd do better closer to people."

My dad looked affectionately at my mom. I wondered after all the years of my mom being crazy how my dad could still look at her like that. He must not see what I see. Then he said, "We're going to wait until spring thaw to move but we want you to know that you're more than welcome to come live with us. If you want to apply for colleges in the area or even find a job, we could work something out."

The thought of living with my parents again was enough to make me take my chances with homelessness in New York. "I don't know what to say," I finally managed. I bit my lip, desperately trying to not say how this move was a giant waste of time and nothing would ever solve my mom's issues. On top of that, Kim and my mom had never gotten along, and putting them in the same zip code was like dropping a nuclear bomb into an active volcano. Talk about scorched earth. No one would survive that!

Dad cut off my train of thought by saying, "So, that's one of your options. We wanted you to know so if you do apply to schools, you are always welcome to live with us." That was his way of wrapping up the conversation, but all I heard was the ticking of the crazy sister bomb waiting to go nuclear.

"That was interesting news," I affirmed. "Sort of a lot to think about. If you don't mind, I'm going to head to my loft to mull this over."

"Go ahead," my dad said. "We got over three feet of snow. We won't be able to leave for the Christmas Day church service tomorrow, but Mom's making homemade chicken and wild rice soup for dinner. I thought we could do gifts right after that. Does that sound okay?"

"I can handle that." I smiled one of those fake toothy smiles. *Two more days. Is it too soon to start counting hours?* The worst thing was, we were so snowed in that even if I wanted to go into town to get a break from this place, I couldn't.

My tiny window was frosted over, creating a shield between the outside world and me. It felt like it was helping to keep me hostage. I had brought my dance bag with a few schoolbooks, thinking I might get bored on the plane. I hadn't, but now even school was a welcomed distraction. It didn't even bother me to do school on Christmas Eve.

I pulled out my language notebook and stared at the title of an overdue required journal entry. We were supposed to journal once a week, but I usually fell asleep when I was only a couple lines into each essay, so I was behind. One of the titles stuck out. "What Am I Thankful For?" Ha-ha! That had to be a joke. I was doing homework on my Christmas vacation, I was snowed in with my crazy parents, I was facing homelessness, my best friends whom I had known my whole life betrayed me, I had a job that worked me to death but didn't pay, and the boy I liked was right across the yard, but he was lost in Candyland!

The only thing that stuck out in my life as something I enjoyed these last few months was the time I spent at Wally's parents' house, particularly the part where I got to talk to Nana about her clothes. That seemed like a pretty pathetic highlight for an eighteen-year-old's life. But I loved those dresses. Especially the Dior. I loved the long lines in the skirt that sucked my eyes right in, reminding me of ballet lines. Without much thought as to what I was doing, I started to sketch her dress on my notebook where my essay was supposed to go. I remembered how the pleats created a wave in the fabric but somehow still laid perfectly flat at the waist.

When I was done with that drawing, I drew another one; creating as my pencil led me. Before I knew it, a couple hours had passed, and I had filled all the blank pages I had reserved for my essays with dresses. It was like I had been in a dress daze when I finally put my book away. Then I noticed the shortness of winter days had already called the sun to start setting and I could smell dinner welcoming me back to the present life. My dad was yelling up to my loft to come down for family time. So, I obediently tucked my book back inside my dance bag, vowed to bite my tongue as well, and went downstairs.

Chapter Twenty-Five

Christmas Day greeted me with sun rays that broke through the frost on my window, warming the side of my cheek until I woke into awareness.

One more day.

I crawled out of bed, forcing my body to move downstairs. My parents were in their same spots as yesterday. That's probably how they spent every day—my dad reading a book, my mom at the stove preparing food.

"Merry Christmas," they both chimed.

"Merry Christmas," I muttered as I poured coffee into a mug then slid into my chair, avoiding eye contact with them. It was amazing to me how fast I had gotten used to living alone and how it was especially hard to have someone in my space in the morning when I wasn't awake as much as I would like to be. I reached to the center of the table for the sugar and poured a good amount into my coffee and stirred it until I no longer saw the little granules.

"The Rogers invited us to their house for Christmas dinner," Dad stated cheerfully. Millie can't wait to see you, and it doesn't make sense for us to make separate meals when we live so close together, so we accepted the invite."

"Oh," I said, unamused. It wasn't that I minded going over there. I would love to see Millie and even Linda. However, I was longing to be back in the city, and I desperately didn't need to see Fulton while I was in an already emotionally vulnerable state. Every second I spent here kept reminding me why I had left.

"They said we can head over anytime if we want to hang out," Dad continued.

"I'm making some homemade buns and a salad to take, and it should be done in about an hour," my mom added.

"We can wait until they are done," my dad agreed, then he turned toward me. "Anything you want to talk about?"

I blinked, drawing a blank. "Nah," I finally said when the silence stretched too long. "Actually, since we're going to go next door, I might take a shower." I got up from the table and headed to the bathroom, welcoming any excuse to hang out by myself.

Linda never failed to impress, even when her canvas was a tiny home. She had decorated the room with white lights, evergreen garland and red velvet bows. "Come on in," she cheerily sang from the kitchen, her eyes obviously searching to meet mine as I followed my parents through the crammed entryway. "Abs, it's so good to see you!" She waited until I was all the way in the room.

"Come, let me hug you." After I gave her a little hug, she pulled away. "You look thin as a rail. Are you eating?" Her eyes scanned me, making me uncomfortable.

"I'm eating but busy with work too."

"Come on in and grab a seat." She had extended their family table to accommodate us, but the caveat was there was officially no walking room. If you wanted to sit at the back of the table, you had to climb over the chairs on your way to get there. She chuckled when she saw us navigate our way to the seats. "Sorry for the lack of space. Next year will be better when we have our new home." She looked assuredly at Eddie, who had also followed us to the table.

"Are you getting a new house?" I asked her as I finally plopped down on my seat.

"Yes, the plan is to build a cabin from sticks. We're starting this spring. Of course, we are going to hire help to make sure it gets done," Eddie explained.

"Was that always the plan?" I asked.

"I think so." Eddie looked at Linda, who gave an affirming nod. "We first wanted to get out here and get the land settled. Now we can focus on our forever home."

"I can't wait to have a kitchen island again," Linda said. "You'll have to make a trip to see it when we get it done." Her eyes landed on my parents.

"We will for sure," my dad said. "There's no way we would forget to visit."

"Where are you guys going?" Fulton asked my dad as he staggered into the room joining us. His hair was matted on the side like he had just got out of bed.

"We are headed to Vermont this spring," Dad explained.

"Really?" Fulton relaxed in his chair. "I didn't know."

"Abs!" Millie squealed from her loft. "I didn't know you were here." She ran down the stairs quickly. I had to do a double take because she had grown a couple inches and looked so big compared to when I saw her last.

"Did you fall asleep?" Linda asked her.

"Yeah, just a little nap," Millie answered before taking a seat next to me.

"She was up all night, waiting for Christmas. I knew she wouldn't make it that long today without crashing," Linda explained while she rummaged through the crammed fridge and took out a bowl with plastic wrap on the top. "Here's a gelatin salad," she said when she placed it in the center of the table next to all the other food. Then she added, "I think we are ready to eat." She squeezed into the last opened chair, and we started a food chain, passing plates around.

"So, Fulton," Dad said when he handed him the corn, "I heard you're trying to get an internship for the summer."

"That's the plan." He scratched the back of his head, like it helped to wake up his brain. "I want to get a lot of hours, so it looks good on my application. I'm transferring next year to see if it helps me get into a vet program. I'm thinking my classes will be even harder next year, and I also need to focus on studying for my GRE. This is the best time to pack in the hours."

"Do you have any ideas where you are applying?" My dad sat back against his chair, fork in hand, but he seemed more interested in Fulton than the meal.

"I have a list of all the vet clinics, and I'm not going to be picky. I'll take whatever I can get."

"That's what I thought, and I was going to tell you if you need a letter of recommendation, I worked with so many vets over the years, I probably know half of them. I could even make a phone call or two if you thought it would help."

"Really?" Fulton blinked a couple of times, before a smile spread wide across his face. "That would be awesome. I'll take all the help I can get."

"Sure. Why don't you send me a list of the places you are applying at, and I'll look it over to see who I know."

"Is it that easy to get him a job?" I asked my dad.

"It's the same thing I did for you."

"Can you get me one that *pays* next time?" I asked a little too sarcastically.

"I can certainly use my connections to help you but remember what we talked about. You're going to need to graduate and gain some more skills, especially if you think you're going to stay in the New York area. It's expensive to live there."

Linda set her fork down, looking over at me. "Do you know what you want to do next year?"

"I don't. I wasn't worried about it either, but dad wants me to have a plan." I didn't want to hash out my failures again in front of the Rogers, so I put my face down and dug into my ham.

Then my mom looked at Fulton and said, "What's your girlfriend think about you transferring schools?"

My ears perked. I didn't know Fulton had told my parents he had a girlfriend.

"She's supportive of me. She knows vet school is competitive, and that I have to do what I need to do."

I couldn't look at his face when he spoke about her. I kept my chin tucked, and I pushed my food around my plate trying to act engrossed.

Then Millie saved the conversation. "Guess what I got for Christmas?" She nudged my arm with her hand, eyes beaming.

"I don't know. What?" I leaned closer to her, acting excited.

"A puppy!"

"What!" I pretended to be shocked. "How come you're only telling me this now and where is he?"

"He's in the shed. Mom said it was too crowded in here today."

"What did you name him?" "His name is Hank."

"That's a great name for a dog." I pretended to be curious about the dog so I wouldn't have to hear about Fulton and his girlfriend. "When do I get to meet him?"

"Now if you want. If you're done eating."

I looked at my plate and somehow, I had managed to clean off most of the food. I set my fork down and looked at Linda. "Do you care if I step out for a second to meet Hank?"

"Nah, go ahead." She waved us toward the door. "I know Millie's been dying to show him to you."

I got up and followed Millie to the entryway, slipped on my boots and coat and went outside, without looking back to ask anyone else to come along. I could handle random small talk and pleasantries, but all the conversation about the future was making my chest tight. I couldn't handle the pressure or the looks telling me to stop stumbling around already and pick a star. A little Millie time was exactly what I needed.

Chapter Twenty-Six

If my trip home did anything good for me, it solidified in my mind what I didn't want to happen after my internship. I didn't want to have to move back with my parents, I didn't want to go to college, and I didn't want to hear about Fulton and his girlfriend anymore! Once I crossed those things off my list, I made a new list that included: finding a job that paid, a cheaper place to rent, and a social life that didn't involve Fulton or his friends.

The timing was perfect too. Since we'd just hired a dozen employees at the store, I was surrounded by women, and we all had one thing in common: fashion. I dove into my work even more and used every opportunity that came my way to look for my next adventure, which only took a couple of months to appear.

"Hey, Abs." Gabby chomped on a grape jellybean while she studied her computer screen.

"Huh?" I placed my finger as a placeholder on an invoice I was checking, then I raised my head so I could see her.

"I met with my accountant last night. We just passed first quarter, and the store's doing phenomenal."

"That's awesome."

"So, I've been having this idea for a while now, and I haven't verbalized it yet because I don't want people to think I'm crazy. However, I feel like I want to tell you, but you have to keep it a secret." She closed her mouth, pinching her lips together so tightly they were turning white.

Now she had my attention. "Sure," I said with my eyes glued to her face. "I can keep a secret."

"I want to open another store," she blurted out.

"I don't think that's crazy at all." I didn't even flinch. "Why would I think you're crazy for that?"

I could see her shoulders narrow in a cringe as she added the next part. "In Paris."

I blinked. "Say what?"

"I know it seems crazy, but the two major fashion cities are New York and Paris. I feel like it's the next step to up my brand. Am I crazy?"

"I don't have a clue about this stuff. Did you ask your accountant?"

"Not about Paris, but the numbers for the store look great, and it's really my only hope of ever going anywhere in this business."

"So, what do you need to do to decide for sure? Can you call someone?"

"Unfortunately, when it's your business, you're the person to call." She gave me a look like she was ready for an adventure. "I'm going there next week. I'm going to look at the retail spaces and see what I would be able to afford."

"Wow, you are serious about this."

"I'm serious about checking to see if there is an opportunity."

I half smiled, thinking it sounded like a huge risk and a ton of work. "Well, I hope it works out for you."

"Do you want to come with?"

I double blinked. "Are you serious?"

"Yeah, I could use someone else to bounce ideas off, and you know my brand as well as anyone since you went through this store opening with me." She leaned closer to me. "Please, I would appreciate it."

"Um, I don't even need to think about that. Yes. I'll come." It was like that statement made time stop. The next week dragged on forever but it did give me something to look forward to, and I stayed busy trying to get ahead in my schoolwork so I wouldn't be behind when I came back.

On the plane, I was too eager to do anything that required much concentration. I don't know how she did it, but Gabby seemed like a cool cucumber, sitting next to me with her ear buds in and an old-school sketch pad, doodling ideas that came to her. "What do you think about one-piece jumpsuits?" she asked.

"Not a fan," I replied without even glancing at her doodle.

"Really? Not any certain style but you just write the whole concept off?"

"Unless you're Cat Woman, I don't think they look good, or comfortable, and they are not that practical for sizing because who is a perfect size on their top and their bottom?"

"That's true about the sizing." She flipped the page on her notebook where she had already started to draw a one-piece suit. "Sometimes I feel like I try so hard to do something different that I go too far. So, what sort of styles are catching your eye these days?"

"Honestly?"

"I wouldn't have asked if I didn't want you to tell me."

"I've been into history lately. When you look back at where we came from, I sort of feel like it's been a race to the bottom. I've recently become so obsessed with vintage Dior."

"Really?" She chuckled. "Where would you wear one of those to?"

"Everywhere. They are so pretty." I pulled out the English notebook from my bag that was stowed under the seat in front of me. "Look, I'll show you how obsessed I am." I flipped through my pages, fanning through the dresses I had drawn over the last few months. "I can't stop drawing them."

Gabby's brows lowered when she looked at my pages. "Interesting." She pointed to a dress I had shaded green with colored pencil. "Look at that collar you put on there."

"It's gorgeous. I love a big heavy collar. It's an accessory all by itself."

She tilted her chin closer to my sketch book, letting her eyes gloss over each dress. "Those are cute."

"You think so?" Getting a compliment from Gabby about my dresses wasn't something I had been fishing for, but boy did it fill my heart with some pride. "I do. There you go." She patted my notebook. "You have your first fashion collection."

It was my turn to chuckle. "Yeah right."

"It is right, and it can be that simple. All you need is one idea. Then you start there. That's what I did. I didn't wake up one day with a whole collection. It takes time. But if you break it down and start with one idea, it's easy."

I let my gaze wander unfocused. After a moment, I asked, "So, if I wanted to make one of these dresses . . ."

"The best thing to do is get the measurements correct to size. I can see they are out of proportion, but that's an easy fix. Then you can either have a sample made or make one yourself. Not that hard anymore."

"Hmm." I didn't say anything more. Any other day I would have dismissed her comments, but I was running low on time. I needed a plan, and nothing else had even remotely piqued my interests. I made a mental note to myself to do more research, and I spent the rest of the flight dreaming up what my own fashion collection would look like.

Chapter Twenty-Seven

"Is that sewer smell?" I whispered to Gabby in the backroom so the realtor wouldn't hear me. This was the sixth place we had looked at today, and each one had been less tempting than the last.

"I can't even think about it, or I'll puke," she replied, pivoted on her heel and waved. "Come on. I'll think of a reason why we need to get out of here fast." She walked back through the door leading to the store space, announcing, "Well, I think we've been able to look at enough today, and I do have some meetings."

The realtor was reading a text message. "Hold on a minute. I got a text from a coworker who is in the process of listing another space. It's fifteen hundred square feet and a block from here but still in the fashion district." She looked up from her phone. "Do you want to see it?"

I was ready to go back to the hotel in defeat, but Gabby jumped at the offer, "Sure."

Walking down the busy commercial street, I noticed a couple of cute stores. The neighborhood wasn't bad at all. The realtor stopped at a white retail building with a large street window. She stuck her key in the lock pad and unlocked it, letting us in. "This is a rare find. It's recently been remodeled. For your store, all you would need to do is add the hardware to the walls."

I knew from the look on Gabby's face that this was the one. It was the only one we had seen all day that was move-in ready, and it had modern updates. Gabby searched the room meticulously, looking everything over. She pointed to the backdoor. "Is there room back there for truck delivery?"

"Let's open it up and check," the realtor said. We walked back while the realtor opened it, revealing a parking pad connected to an alley.

"This looks great," Gabby declared when she stepped outside. "We won't have any problem getting a truck in here."

"This is better than our New York location," I affirmed.

Gabby's confidence in this location was evident with the direct eye contact she made with the realtor when she said, "I've seen enough to know this is a great find, and I'd love to apply for it."

"Perfect. We'll go back inside and get the paperwork started."

Later that night after we got done with our application papers, we walked into a restaurant. "I'm starving," Gabby said.

I hung my bag over the back of a barstool and sat. "Me too," I said. A waitress came over and left us waters and menus. I skimmed the salads, looking for the word *poulet*. I didn't know French, but I was pretty sure that meant chicken.

The waitress came back, and I pointed to a salad on the menu. She nodded at me, then turned to Gabby, who pointed to something on the menu too. Then the waitress took our menus and left. I slid my water cup closer to me and smelled it—the water smelled different here. I thought about drinking it but instead commented, "I thought it would be harder to get around without the language, but so far it seems they are used to Americans."

Gabby was reading something on her phone again and didn't reply. I looked around the place, letting my eyes land on the window and watched the numerous shoppers walking by. After a moment, Gabby put her phone face down on the table and looked at me. "Sorry, I was reading an email from Lexi."

"Everything okay?" I asked.

"Yeah. It sounds like everything's great. She's so good for that store. The best decision I ever made was hiring her. I'm not worried one bit that I can't be there right now. I hope I can find someone equally qualified to run the store here."

"It might be a bigger challenge especially with the language barrier," I said, still gazing out the window.

"I've already decided to learn French, so hopefully after I live here a few months, it will be easier," she replied.

Her comment jolted me a little and I refaced my attention on her. "You're moving here?"

"I'm going to have to while the store is being built, and depending on who I hire, maybe even longer."

"I had no idea," I said, then paused because our waitress came back with our salads. I opened my napkin and set it on my lap, picked up my fork, and took my first bite. "Hmm, that's yummy."

Gabby chewed her first bite too, then swallowed and said, "It is good." She took a sip of her water, then paused before taking another bite. "So, what are your plans for after you graduate?"

"You sound like my dad."

"I'm not trying to be nosey," she insisted. "I just know we had an agreement for this internship until school was over, and it's coming up. What do you have left of school—a few weeks?"

"I want to be done by the middle of May, so maybe six weeks."

"Have you thought about what you are going to do?"

"Sort of. I mean, I've thought a lot about it. My dad said he would only help me if I'm in school. If I decide to work, then I must be able to support myself. I think he's doing that to motivate me to get more schooling, but I don't see the point. I don't learn from books. I learned way more in this internship than I did in all of high school."

Gabby's head bounced up and down in agreement. "You do learn more your first year working than you do in all your schooling, even if you go to college. They can't teach you real life, especially if you become an entrepreneur."

"So, what do you think I should do?" I put my fork down so I could think. "I mean, you know what's available more than I do. Do I need college?"

"It depends on what you want to do. What do you want to do?"

I shrugged my shoulders. "It's hard to say because I don't know what all the jobs are. I know what I don't like to do. I don't want to do sales or retail. I love working with clothes, but I don't like to sew. I'd love to design like you, but then I have to go back to school, and I don't want to. Really, the only thing that excites me right now are vintage dresses." I let out a heavy sigh.

"What if there was a way for you to learn design without going to school?"

"What do you mean?" I asked, her question definitely piquing my interest.

"Before there were colleges, most people learned by apprenticeships. What if you and I worked something out where you could continue to work for me, but instead of being my assistant, you would be moved into a design role as my design apprentice where I could train you?"

"How is that different than an internship?" I pondered out loud.

"It's probably not much different. But I'm trying to think of a way your dad would help support you on something like that. It could be an opportunity of a lifetime, if you ask me. Most people have to pay to go to college. I can teach you for free, but I can't afford to pay you. You would need your dad's financial support."

"It sounds great . . ." I agreed, still wondering how I would get my dad to agree to paying for me to *not* go to school for another year. Relief welled in my chest, telling me that I might have more time before I had to find a job, but I was confused as to why she would go through all the trouble, so I asked, "What would be in it for you then?"

"I was thinking about this on the plane already," she admitted.

"You were thinking about this earlier?" I questioned.

"I was. When I saw your designs, I knew that was your talent. I was trying to think of a way to help you. You have been a tremendous help to me, and I'll be honest, I'm going to hate to lose you as my assistant. I started to think there had to be a way where we could both benefit from an arrangement. I thought if you wanted to stay working as my assistant part time for free, then I could train you in design as payment."

"I don't know what to say. I can't think of a reason not to say yes."

She held up her hand to stop me. "Talk to your dad about it first. See if he can help you, because it would be a lot of hours between the assistant work and then adding in the apprenticeship position, and again, I wouldn't be paying you. Your dad would still need to help with bills. And, just because I'm adding in the apprentice position doesn't mean I need less assistance. I'm going to be super busy these next months with the store in New York and then moving and opening a new store. It's going to be a lot of hours."

"Wait a second." I felt my eyebrows knit together. "How will you train me if you are moving?"

"You're going to have to move too." She took a sip of her water, then added, "If you want the experience. I can't change my business plans to suit your need. I'd love to have you help me, but you're going to need to be here with me."

My stomach did a pirouette! I've never felt like this before. I had a flashback of my dad telling me to look at the stars I can see and pick one. I'm pretty sure my heart just picked it. *I was going to move to Paris!* Now, all I had to do was convince my dad that I didn't need to go to college.

Chapter Twenty-Eight

"How was your trip?" My dad's voice greeted me on the phone the day after I got back.

I locked the door to my studio behind me and then adjusted my phone on my ear. "It was great. Actually, too great. Something came up that I need to talk to you about."

"Sounds expensive." I could hear the smile in my dad's tone.

"Maybe . . ." I hesitated but knew I had to be honest and straight forward, so I continued, "Gabby and I were talking about what I wanted to do after my internship, and I don't even know how it happened, but she offered me an apprentice designer position where she said she would train me if I continued to do part-time assisting. It's like a trade. It seems like a lot of free work on my end, but she assured me that it was a great deal. I would learn a lot, and I would probably not need college. What do you think?"

"So, you would work for free in exchange for more advanced training?"

"I think so," I said. "She said she can train me to do the designing I would normally have to pay to go to school for. Does that sound weird to you?"

"No, not necessarily . . . it sounds like it could be a great offer. My concern would be that she would need structure and real goals. I wouldn't want it to be like it is now where you show up and get thrown into stuff and maybe you learn something or maybe you don't. Gabby can be sort of scattered."

"I could see it being very random," I said, knowing he was spot on about Gabby.

"I would ask her to help you put together a plan with dates and goals for what you want to learn. Tell her *I* need it. If she could commit to something like that, then I'd be all in for supporting you. It could be the next step for you toward a successful career."

I chewed my lip while I thought and all of a sudden, my mind was flooded with doubt. I wasn't sure if this was the career I even wanted. Everything was happening at such a rocket-speed pace my mind couldn't keep up. However, it seemed like a better deal than enrolling in college and having to pay for a program. "What are you thinking?" my dad probed.

"It seems rushed that I have to decide today what I want to do with the rest of my life."

"It's not really the rest of your life," he reassured me. "You just need a plan for right now. I'd like to see you exploring something to help you gain advanced job skills. You have a choice. If you have a better option somewhere else, don't hesitate to bring it up."

"That's just it. I don't have another option. It seems like my choice is decided for me because this is the only thing that I have."

"Well, then, maybe it's meant to be. I think you'd be great at it. You get along well with Gabby. It won't be a forever gig, but it can help take you to your path."

"It's just so different than what I was thinking would happen. Oh, the thing I forget to mention is that Gabby has to move to open her store. If I want to accept her offer, I have to move with her to Paris." I held my breath, waiting for my dad to freak out, but surprisingly I heard a lighter air in his voice.

"Paris? Wow. What an amazing opportunity to see the industry from there and with Gabby. It will be a great resume builder. Sounds exciting."

"Really?"

"Yeah, I think so. You worked hard this year. If this is what you want to do next year, I'm happy to help you. I'll have to research a little to see what the expenses are, but we can work out a budget and go from there."

"You mean, you're really going to be okay with me moving to Paris?" I wished I had video chatted him because I wanted to see his facial expression to know he wasn't kidding.

"I am. Remember, I wanted you to have a plan. As long as you are working towards something, you are going forward."

I remembered the plan speech. Pick a star and stumble toward it. The more I thought about it, the more I didn't see myself doing anything else. I began to feel strongly about my decision to accept Gabby's job offer. So, when the last lingering signs of winter became harder to spot, like the icy cool water droplets dripping from the leaves of a crab tree or a patch of ground a little too bare because the spring foliage hadn't grown in yet, I knew I was ready for my next adventure. I accepted her position and started to plan for my move. Before I knew it, I had one last weekend left in the city, and my bags were packed.

Then, like a fresh spring surprise, I got an unexpected text from Fulton.

Fulton: *I heard you got a new job offer in Paris. Congrats!*

Me: *Thanks. I'm sort of terrified.*

Fulton: *I was wondering if you wanted to come with me to Wally's show tonight. Sort of a last night out before you ship out.*

I cringed. I knew he meant well by including me in his life with his friends, but I didn't care to tag along. I hadn't seen him since Christmas, and I had been doing well with my feelings toward him. It didn't bother me anymore, and I sort of preferred to leave my feelings unstirred.

Me: *I don't know if I feel like it. I've got a lot of stuff to do before then.*

Fulton: *Okay. How about an early dinner? You have to eat.*

I checked my watch. It was already past three, and if he had plans to go to the theatre, then I knew it would be quick. I felt the familiar tug of hunger in my stomach trying to answer for me.

Me: *Sure. What time are you thinking?*

Fulton: *Can you be ready by six?*

Me: *Sure.*

Fulton: *I'll meet you at your place.*

Me: *Okay.*

I set my phone down. For the first time all day, I took note that I still looked like I had just crawled out of bed. I walked to my closet, and right away my eyes were drawn to the dress I had made with Gabby earlier that week. We had joked it was a "Gabby by Abby" design. It was completely reminiscent of a vintage Dior. It was a jewel-toned blue and had a skirt fit for a princess. It wasn't perfect, but I was proud of it. A smile crept into my lips as I thought about wearing my dress out in public. It was obviously too much dress for a casual dinner, but I couldn't help but wish I could wear it tonight as I reached passed it and snatched my favorite pair of jeans. The forecast said it was going to rain later tonight too, so I made sure to set my umbrella by the door. Then I grabbed my shower caddy and a towel and headed to the bathroom, ready to celebrate my last night in New York.

Flashing his laid-back smile at me when I walked down the stairs, Fulton greeted me, "Hey stranger." I tried hard not to notice that he was wearing a nice shirt, *like a really nice shirt* that didn't even have a college logo on it.

"Hey yourself." I joined him on the sidewalk, and our steps fell into unison toward Midtown. "Where are we going?"

"You can pick if you have a preference, but I was able to get us reservations at the Greek place I was supposed to take you to for your birthday. I thought I would make it up to you. Do you want to go there?"

I looked at him suspiciously. "How'd you get a reservation on a Saturday night?"

His smile got even more relaxed. "I know people."

"Oh, you're like a celebrity then?"

He chuckled. "Nah, not even close. Griz started working there as an assistant manager, so he hooked me up."

"Oh, good for him. Does he like it?"

"He does," Fulton chatted away as we walked. "He studied restaurant management. He only had a two-year program, so he's graduating, and it's a good first job for him."

"I can't believe it's been two years since you started there, and you're graduating. What about you? What's next?" I asked.

"I'm actually transferring to Stony Brook next fall. They have a pre-vet program, and I'll have a better chance of getting into vet school if I get my undergrad from there."

"Very cool."

"So actually, for the summer, you're going to die to hear this but I'm going to go stay in Montana to save money."

I let my mouth fall into a dramatic gasp. "You've come down with a brain-eating disease that has taken all your sanity?"

"I thought that might be your reaction." His smile got wider. "But yeah, my parents are building their new cabin, and I'm going to stay in your old place since your parents moved. My dad scouted out a bunch of trees I can cut for firewood to sell to the locals for money. And it's really only ten weeks, so I should survive."

"I thought you wanted an internship?"

"I did until I realized that an internship at my level would mean more poop scooping. I can do that on the farm for free without having to pay high city rent."

"Chopping firewood all summer. Hmm."

"It's not as glamourous as moving to Paris to study design, but we can't all have your fabulous life." He gave me a little jab with his elbow.

"Funny," I said with a hint of sarcasm, then added in a more serious tone, "I don't think my life is glamorous, but I have worked my butt off to get this opportunity." I took a deep breath, appreciating the moment, but it must have fueled my bravery because I then asked, "So, what does Candace think of you being in Montana all summer?"

He gave me one of those looks my grandma used to give me when she couldn't remember my name but she knew she recognized my face. "Oh, we aren't together anymore," he finally said. Then he added, "We broke up months ago—pretty much right after Christmas."

I felt my eyes widen but I tried to hide my interest by staring forward. "You did. How come?"

"You know," his voice was sort of light and airy, not at all like someone sad about a breakup, "there really wasn't a reason to break up, but it was more that I couldn't think of a reason to stay together, especially since I knew I was moving."

"That sounds sort of harsh."

"You think so?" His head tilted while he thought, then he said, "I didn't mean it to be harsh. I think we were always good friends. At least from my perspective. It made sense for us to try dating since we saw each other all the time and got along well. I would never say a bad thing about her. She's great, but I sort of always felt like we were better friends."

"So, you friend-zoned her." I tried to lift the mood by making a joke, but I could tell he didn't receive it as a joke.

"I don't think it was like that. This last semester we didn't have any classes together, so we didn't have to be around each other, and we naturally drifted. It wasn't intentional, but once we didn't have all our classes, we didn't have much in common."

I bobbed my head, taking in the seriousness of his tone. "Wally once said something like if you don't think about them when they are not there, then they are probably not the one. That kind of sounds like what happened to you."

The look on his face strained like he had taken a bite of mystery meat, and he was hoping it was chicken but had a hint that it might have been roadkill. "Wally told you that?"

"I know, right?" I chuckled. "Pretty serious stuff coming from him, but we had a good chat about his female friend."

"Ah." He bowed his head like he was relieved to learn the meat actually was, in fact, chicken and it was okay to proceed. "Honestly," he said as his shoulders visibly loosened, "I haven't thought much about it. Like I said, we tried, and it was fine but nothing worth trying to hold onto over long distance. I've been so busy with school and clinic hours I haven't had much time to think about anything else. Then I talked to my mom this morning. She said you were getting ready to leave the city, and it sort of . . . surprised me." His voice got slow the last few words like he didn't know where he was going with his thought.

"Not for good, just for a while," I corrected him.

"And then?" he asked.

"And then . . . I'll have to see." I didn't mean to look at him then, but we had walked right up to the outside of the restaurant. It was a reflex for me to turn to make sure we were going to go inside together, but the look he gave me back made me stop dead in my tracks. I'm pretty sure I remembered seeing that look on his face before. It was when we were ten and our parents had let us stand in line for nine hours outside the bookstore waiting for the release of the next novel of his favorite series. Right when we got to the front of the line, they ran out of books. The disappointment was mind-blowing. It was that moment and that look that was flashing before me now, and it cemented my feet to the ground. *Fulton was disappointed.*

A couple walked past us with their arms linked together, and it seemed to play in slow motion. I could feel the heaviness of my feet rising. It was like a thaw slowly started to happen in my feet, but the thaw activated an emotion that had been frozen. The thaw kept moving to my body and made its way into my heart, and then *wham*, I was reminded I had feelings for Fulton! The crazy thing was that it didn't stop there. It flowed up, warming my face, and I felt my cheeks blush. I lowered my eyes to avoid looking at him because now, for some reason, I was embarrassed like a schoolgirl. I tried to shake it off by asking, "Should we go in?" He agreed by extending his arm, inviting me to walk first. Then I swallowed, and took a step forward, praying, *Please don't embarrass yourself, Abs.*

Chapter Twenty-Nine

Despite how crammed the restaurant was, the host easily found us a table in a quaint corner. Earlier, as I was getting ready to meet Fulton, I had a nonchalant attitude toward this dinner. I didn't know then that Fulton was single, and I had even half expected Candace to tag along. *Everything had changed now.* I was intensely aware that I was leaving the city in a couple of days, and for the first time in my life, I had no idea when I would see Fulton again.

I gave my menu to the waiter after he took our order and then turned to look at Fulton. He smiled at me briefly with one of those smiles of someone you meet while passing the street, then his attention slipped away. His passing smile hit me hard. It wasn't my nature to get wrapped up in my feelings, and maybe it was my impending move, but I had a hard time looking casual. I tucked my chin down and pretended to study the dessert menu.

"What's wrong?" he asked when his eyes finally landed back on me.

"Nothing's *wrong*. I just have a lot on my mind. It's hard to shut it down," I replied truthfully.

"Are you nervous about the move?"

"No, not really. Maybe. I'll pretty much be doing the same job but in a different city. I don't expect I'll have much time to enjoy Paris anyway. So, no, that's not really bothering me."

"It shouldn't. You're going to have a blast and learn so much. Time will fly," he replied. I was hoping he would follow up with asking me what was bothering me again, but it wasn't Fulton's nature to pry. He always had more of a quietness about him. It wasn't self-centeredness or lack of empathy. It was his way of being, and it usually succeeded in making me want to open up to him.

"So, I was thinking." I lightly licked my lips, hoping it would make the words easier. "This is the first experience in my life that you won't be a part of."

His green eyes brightened like they synchronized with the images in my head of us going through every childhood experience together and even keeping tabs on each other over the last year while we lived our own separate adult lives but in the same city. He slowly raised and lowered his chin. "That's true. We have been there for every awkward stage and all the embarrassing stuff in the middle."

"And even when I come home from Paris to visit, it won't be near you since my folks are moving."

He nodded again. "Yeah, it is kind of strange to think about. I don't think we'll ever run into each other unintentionally again." His gaze floated to the side, and our waiter came to the table with our food. He spread his napkin and took a couple bites. When a pleased upward curl of the corners of his mouth crept over his face to signify his enjoyment of his food, I realized he wasn't going to add anything to his comment, and it tugged at my heart. Tonight, was potentially goodbye *forever*.

There was a dizziness in my brain replaying all the mean things I had said to him over the years, and the times I had made fun of him behind his back to Tina and Becky. Why he ever befriended me after the way I treated him was beyond me. The images in my brain kept coming. I saw all his birthday parties I had been dragged to and how I had been mortified to be there. I saw all the dance recitals he had attended and again how embarrassed I had been to see him attend with his parents. I saw him passing me in the halls at school and how I looked away, pretending to not see him. All these images buzzed in my brain like a hive of angry bees. I wondered how I could have been so wrong and missed him when it had mattered. It could have been so different had I only got over myself sooner. I had completely wasted what could have been the relationship of a lifetime because I was spoiled and stuck up.

"Are you okay?" Fulton's words made my mind replant on the present.

"Yeah. Why?" I shoveled my loaded fork into my mouth, trying to hide the shame I had dug up.

"Your face is, like, blanched. I'm wondering if I should scoot my chair over so you don't hit me when you hurl up all your food."

I lowered my lashes. "It can't be that bad."

"For real." He tilted his head to the exit behind us. "You want to step outside for some air?"

It was like my lungs had ears, and as soon as he said it, they deflated to get some attention. "Actually," I sat on the edge of my seat, now focused on the door too, "I think I'm ready to go."

His forehead lined and his lips quietly parted, and then he softly said, "Sure."

I took measured breaths, and I waited for the next few minutes to pass while we paid. Outside, I was waiting for the fresh air to rejuvenate my lungs with the kick they craved, but it didn't work. I still lacked . . . something.

Fulton motioned to a bench. "Maybe you should sit before we walk?"

I shook my head. I knew moving would calm me faster. "We can walk."

"I didn't look at it, but maybe your chicken wasn't cooked well," Fulton offered as we moved slowly back in the direction of my place. He kept staring over at me like he was ready for me to barf at any moment.

My eyes were unable to even glance in his direction. In a moment we would be at my house. I'd have to say goodbye to him, but a different goodbye—a forever goodbye.

His growing concern was evident through the deepening lines on his brow. "You want me to grab a cab?"

"No, I just need a moment to collect my thoughts."

"Will you tell me what's wrong?"

I felt my lips cave downward, knowing I had to get *something* off my chest. I didn't know how, so I just let the words come out. "I used to be really mean to you, wasn't I?"

The expressiveness of his eyes clouded with protectiveness. "Why are you bringing that up?"

"I can't not think about it. It's like as soon as I realized this could be the last time I'd ever see you, I couldn't stop thinking about how terrible I was to you and how I had maybe wasted what could have been something . . . else." With the brave eyes I used in the past to look at the packed auditorium of a ballet audience, I waited for him to turn his eyes toward mine.

He didn't waver or give me any reason to shift my attention, so I held onto his gaze and silently prayed he didn't need me to explain anything more. I didn't think my heart could handle any more shame than what it already felt.

"You can be pretty fierce," he stated gently with his eyes still locked in communion with mine. Then broke our gaze to watch where we were walking. "Do you remember the first time I saw you?"

I let out a light breath of respite when he changed the conversation, relieving me of the shame I felt. "Um, I remember coming to your place in Midtown. Let's see . . . I think I had to be maybe four. I know I wasn't in school. So, you were probably six?" I paused as I pulled the memory from the back of my brain. "I remember you hid upstairs under your bed the whole time I was there. I wanted to play but you refused to come down. I could see you peeking out every once in a while, from underneath your bed, but you never got off the floor." I smirked at the thought of how silly that moment felt now.

"I remember that. But that's not the first time I saw you." His voice treaded softly. "My parents had dragged me to your dance recital the week before."

"Ah." I nodded. "You've been to more of my dance recitals than anyone else, including both of my parents."

"I remember I cried because I thought dance was stupid and I didn't want to go. I wanted to go to a superhero movie with my cousins instead."

I felt my lips tighten and curl upward. "I'm sorry. The pains of childhood."

"But I watched you dance because my parents made me, and I hated it. I sulked about how stupid it was and how you were a dumb girl I didn't want to watch."

I chuckled lightly and then said, "Wow, thanks. That makes me feel special."

His voice didn't lighten, and he continued in all seriousness. "Then about halfway through the show, you fell."

I knew exactly the moment he was talking about. "I had problems with my ankles back then too," I added.

"But you didn't flinch," he went on. "You got up; you had this fierce look on your face like you were going to master that dance if it meant you had to die dancing."

"I always took dance seriously," I agreed, remembering the most embarrassing moment of my life at that age. Oddly I saw it differently now that I knew how that moment had shaped future moments in my life in how I approached failure—I never accepted it. It had been a defining moment for sure. "I remember that fall. It's crazy to think back on how young I was, but I did handle it well."

"I watched you fall, but it was in the moments after, when you got up, that I felt something was different about you. It's hard to explain, but I knew you were a force. As little as you were, even back then . . . but you haven't changed." Then he smiled at me, amused. "And maybe that's why I hid under the bed. I was afraid of you."

I let out a small chuckle with the air left in my lungs and smiled sweetly at him. "You were never afraid of me." He shrugged his shoulders like he wasn't going to tell his secret. We were at my building now, and we sort of hovered in front of the door. I didn't want to say goodbye, but it felt so insanely awkward hanging out on the sidewalk with people passing by. "Did I ever show you the view of the city from the rooftop of my dormitory?" I asked.

"I don't think you have." He raised a curious eyebrow. "Is that an invitation?"

"Yeah, you should come on up." I turned, leading the way upstairs. "It has to be one of the best kept secrets of the city," I explained.

"I don't think the New York City skyline ever gets old."

"No, especially at night," I agreed.

We arrived on the empty roof top together, but he continued to meander until he was all the way to the edge, looking over. "Wow, this is breathtaking," Fulton called back to me. "This would be a great place to come to do some thinking."

"It totally is," I agreed, taking a place next to him. Looking down below at the city of millions of people—all bustling like tiny dots moving in their own directions—it made me feel sort of mysterious, clandestinely hiding above it all. It was that perfect time of night when the sun had set and the building lights had started to come on, emitting a brilliant glow. If the city lights weren't enough, a couple of stray stars were peeking out from a cloud, reminding me of when my dad had told me to pick a star. Then I had a probing thought: *What if maybe Fulton was one of those stars I was meant to pick.*

Then like he was reading my mind, he lightly elbowed me to get my attention. Looking intrigued, he asked, "So, can you tell me more about what you think it is that you wasted?"

Most of me wanted to hide and deny I had said that, but there was a glimmer inside my heart, urging me to be honest or I'd regret it. "I . . . I was thinking about how you said it had made sense for you to *date* Candace."

He waited silently for me to continue, which sort of killed me a little because I really didn't want to have to clarify what I was thinking, but I went on: "I was thinking about why it never made sense for us to try . . . dating, but it made me remember how mean I was to you. Then, I knew why it never made sense. But now we get along well . . . but I'm moving so it definitely won't ever make sense . . ." I fumbled through my thoughts, hoping I wouldn't have to explain it even more.

His eyes blazed with curiosity. "Are you trying to say you wished we would have tried dating?"

I dug my teeth so far down into my lip, I wanted to cry, but it was the only thing I could do to prevent myself from screaming. Then I forced myself to keep eye contact even though I felt myself blushing. "Did you ever think about that?"

"Are you being serious right now or is that the bad chicken talking?"

I searched his face for clues to how he was receiving this confession, but his face was difficult to read. I knew if I didn't at least hint toward my feelings, I would hate myself, but I desperately wanted him to make this easier for me by giving me a clue. Thankfully, my silence must have been enough to let him know I was serious, and his face softened, making his eyes noticeably gentle. "I always knew you were out of my league," he said in a voice barely above a whisper.

"Never thought about it?" I repeated, needing confirmation.

He raised his eyebrows. "Like, this is a real question for you? You're totally serious?"

I could feel my face tighten nervously, like I was waiting for a twelve-inch needle to stab me with a shot. "I am," I squeaked out. But it was just like my bad luck that I felt the first few drops of a light drizzle tickle the tips of my chin. Glad for a distraction, I grabbed my trusted umbrella, opened it and left enough room for Fulton to stand under it too. We didn't talk at all while I did this, and I could feel my hand shaking the whole time. Now I was left standing to close to him, staring.

I saw his shoulders rise, taking a deep breath and then I watched them fall as he let it out slowly. It seemed to take forever, and I knew he was stalling and trying to think of a way to tell me I was crazy and that we could never date because I was a mean girl. I knew I had gone *way* too far by bringing this up and I would forever feel humiliated about this moment. Then I remembered it would be okay because I was moving. I would never have to see him again! Fulton interrupted my thoughts by saying, "So, as I said, I always knew you thought I was a geek, so I never really went there." He paused long enough to let his eyes pierce into my heart, which was already feeling rejection. It actually was less of a piercing and more of a slaying—yep, I was dying. Then he continued, "But, if I were being honest, as I saw you change in Montana, I did start to like who you were changing into, but I never thought about it much because I always got a not-interested vibe from you."

"So, you never considered it," I said flatly, ready to dismiss the topic as I felt my cheeks burn red hot and I focused on my dying—just a couple more minutes of this humiliation and I would bleed out right here on the roof.

His eyes narrowed, like he might also be feeling a little shy when he said, "Like I said, I just always knew you were out of my league." Then his eyes widened—more serious this time—toward me. "What about you? Do you think about it?"

I looked above his head because I didn't want to see the rejection in his eyes. I wanted to lie and say I was just making conversation, but I was almost already dead so I figured I might as well finish the job. "I never thought about it, *ever*, while we were in high school. But then there was that night we said goodbye in Montana. I remember feeling scared you were leaving, and that confused me." I blinked a couple times, still focusing on the top of his head. "Then I was excited to move back here to see if we could connect again, but everything was so confusing." I snuck a peek at his face, then quickly looked down, but not before I could see his eyes squint a little like the sun was too bright, even though there wasn't any sun.

Then he said, "Wait a second. So, this isn't like a new thought you had. You had these thoughts back then?"

Yep, I was going to die today. His direct question pierced my chest again, and I felt my already bludgeoned heart stop. I tried to downplay my confession by saying, "I think I was more confused back then." He looked at me like he knew I was holding back, so I added, "But then I started to think about it maybe—like, *in November*."

"November?" His jaw dropped. "Why didn't you say something?"

I threw my hands up. This conversation was too hard. "You were with Candace."

"Ah." He ran his hand through his hair, causing it to become slightly disheveled in the front.

I could feel my heart *racing* again, which gave me hope that I had another life. I decided that to try to salvage this life I had to take back my confession. "I'm sorry. I'm totally embarrassed that I even said anything because you obviously aren't even close to—"

He reached out and touched my arm lightly. His eyes were both unafraid and affectionate. "It's okay," he said. Questions and random words raced through my head, but I didn't let them out. I needed him to say something—anything that took the pressure off me—but he didn't talk. He just looked at me and let his lips curl into one of those brilliant smiles steeped with wonder that he sometimes gets.

"You have to say something." I groaned, needing words to confirm what was happening.

"Shh, just wait a second."

"Are you shushing me?" My nerves were still in overdrive and I could feel myself wanting to giggle, but I held it in. I didn't know why I was so nervous, but it was like weird giddy nervousness and I wanted to die all over again. If it was possible, I was going to die twice today.

"I need to give myself a second," he finally said. "It feels unreal."

"Sorry to just spring that on you like that," I started to ramble. "I know it doesn't make sense for us to try dating, but I couldn't really hold in—"

"It makes sense," he interrupted me in a soft voice.

"How?" I fumbled, suspending my belief that a relationship could be possible. "I'm *moving* to Paris in two days."

"I don't know how it makes sense . . ." His eyes penetrated mine, and I was no longer afraid of them. "Somehow, it sort of feels like it makes the most sense."

"You really think so?" I squeaked out.

"I mean, it *sucks* that you are moving right away so we don't really have time to figure anything out, but . . . but I don't think it's a reason to not try. You are not going to be there forever, and I can come visit you."

"You're going to come visit me?" It was my turn to look at him suspiciously because this was happening so fast. I had pretty much given up hope that we would ever have this conversation, let alone actually be together, but it seemed like that was what he was saying. I wanted him to say the words, but when I looked at him, I didn't need them anymore, because the smile he gave me told me he was all in and it poured into my heart in a space that felt like it had been reserved for him. Like in a movie, the drizzling stopped, and I let my umbrella fall to the ground so I could step closer to him. He reached his arms out, and I walked right into a warm hug. My heart fluttered hard in my chest, as it felt amazing to be his arms. I inhaled a deep breath, and was letting out slowly when oddly, he chuckled.

"Why are you laughing?" I asked.

"I just had the most morbid thought." His grin was sort of rascally but sweet at the same time, making me completely confused.

"Now? What is morbid now?"

He shook his head like he wanted me to ignore his ill-timed laughter.

Then my heart constricted again, getting worried that I had read him wrong. I pressed him, "Tell me what you would laugh about right now."

"I was thinking how lucky I am, and then it popped into my head that I was glad our parents made us homestead in Montana—if that's the extreme it took to get us here. So, I felt grateful for Montana. Then I laughed at how absurd that felt to admit."

I giggled slowly, scoffing at the praise of our homestead adventure, but I immediately rescinded when I realized he was right. It did take moving all the way to the sticks to open my heart enough to deserve someone like Fulton, and I was lucky too. I shook my head in disbelief to foreshadow what I was about to confess, and I said, *"Thank God for Montana."*

About J.P. Sterling

J.P. Sterling grew up watching old reruns of Lucille Ball and Mary Tyler Moore and fell in love with wholesome entertainment and slapstick comedy. She loves leaning into the over-the-top humor and full circle moments, especially if it means the underdog gets to shine.

Aside from writing, she's also a wife and homeschooling mom, a holistic dietitian, a former college professor and lover of all-things dark chocolate.

*No swears. Just kisses. No Blasphemies. *

Let's get social!

Hey you amazing reader! You are invited to join my private reader group for all-things clean books and friends.

Enter the group here:

https://www.facebook.com/groups/1500850764081965

Other places to follow me:

Instagram:

https://www.instagram.com/stories/authorjpsterling/

Facebook: https://www.facebook.com/jpsterlingauthor/

Amazon:

https://www.amazon.com/stores/author/B01N9TJXJN/about

Also by J.P. Sterling

<u>Christmas Shenanigans (All Standalones)</u>

Mingle All the Way

Tis the Season to Get Married

Let's Not and Sleigh We Did

<u>The Coffee Loft Series (All Standalones)</u>

Pardon My French Press

No More Mr. Chia Guy

Truly, Madly, Steeply Brew

<u>Sweet Hockey RomCom (All Standalones)</u>

The Pucker-Up Pact

Shot Through the Heart

Come and Get Your Glove (Coming 2025)

<u>A Modern Fairy Tale Series (All Standalones)</u>

Royally Rugged

<u>Bosses and Billionaires Series (All Standalones)</u>

Maid for my Billionaire Boss

Upcycling My Rig-Pig Boss

Kissed by My Billionaire Boss

Marooned with My Celebrity Boss

A Heart that Dances Series (A New Adult Series)

Dancing on Broken Ankles

The Stars We See

A Heart that Dances

A Heart that Loves

Water and Stone Duet (A coming-of-age Series)

Ruby in the Water

Lily in the Stone

www.ingramcontent.com/pod-product-compliance
Lightning Source LLC
Chambersburg PA
CBHW021654110726
47902CB00007B/1929